P9-DFJ-322

THE CHASE

Three or four times, I stumbled. Rocks and cactus cut through my pants, left my knees bloody, but I didn't stay down long. I'd jump up, keep footing it, winding along the draw, my brogans pushing hard into the sand. Sweating. My throat parched. Knowing my feet would be bad blistered before long.

I ran.

The ringing of metal hoofs on the rocks sang out behind me, thundering, and I screamed like a little girl, knowing somebody on horseback came after me, knowing I could never outrun horse or mule. I saw this grove of yucca, weaved in and out of it, hoping that would slow down my pursuer, and I reckon it did, but then I was back out in the open, running down a little hill, hearing the pounding hoofs draw closer, could hear the horse snorting, the rider cursing, and then felt the horse and rider right beside me, and I yelled out again, expecting a bullet in my spine, tried to duck, but a hand gripped my shirt, lifted me up, and I was tossed, smashed into the rocks, and figured I was dead.

Soldier's Farewell

Johnny D. Boggs

LEISURE BOOKS NEW YORK CITY

For Henry W. Allen,
whom I wish I had known,
alias Will Henry, alias Clay Fisher,
whom I know pretty well.

A LEISURE BOOK®

July 2010

Published by special arrangement with Golden West Literary Agency.

Dorchester Publishing Co., Inc.
200 Madison Avenue
New York, NY 10016

ISBN 10: 0-8439-6416-2
ISBN 13: 978-0-8439-6416-5

Visit us online at www.dorchesterpub.com.

Prologue

July 25, 1865

"And Cain talked with Abel his brother," the verse in Genesis reads, "and it came to pass, when they were in the field, that Cain rose up against Abel his brother. . . ."

For four years now, that bit of Scripture has been echoing through my head. Four years, better than four, actually, I've envisioned myself playing the rôle of Cain, justifying premeditated murder.

I am not my brother's keeper. Nobody could keep a tight rein on Julian Munro. Not me. Not even Pa.

Four years of hatred, abomination for my own flesh and blood, four years of torment. Four years watching this miserable stagecoach station in the middle of nowhere turn to dust, watching me mutate into fugitive and vagabond. Four years waiting for a war to end, waiting for my older brother to dare show his face—never once accepting the fact that he could very well have been slain by some enemy's bullet, by grapeshot, or fever, or . . . maybe . . . a broken heart.

No, for four years it has been written in my own broken, blackened heart that it would be me who rose up against my brother.

". . . and slew him."

Hard words, I've been told. Bitter words. Wrong words. Too much for a boy not even 17.

"The devil owns this place," Tori pleaded with

me. "Always, it is cursed. It kill you, too, if you no leave. Get out, Smith. Get out! Please, for God's sake, you must go, for your own sake!"

She had been crying when she said all that. The last time I saw her, close to a year and a half ago. Strong words, perhaps even the right words, coming from a young girl's mouth, but, like me, she had been forced to grow up quickly. Lieutenant Julian Munro had seen to that.

If you're reading this note stuck inside this diary, you have arrived at Soldier's Farewell. Not much to look at, is there? You're at North Latitude 32°, 21 minutes, 23 seconds, West Longitude 108°, 22 minutes, 16 seconds—we learned that from Pa—or, once, what seems like a lifetime ago, 33 1/2 hours from Franklin to the east and 41 hours from Tucson to the west—Mr. John Butterfield had chiseled those numbers into our heads. That had been during the running of the Overland Mail Company along the old Ox-Bow Route, from Tipton, Missouri, all the way to San Francisco, California, twice-a-week (each way) mail and passenger service covering 2,800 miles in less than 25 days.

The Ox-Box's no more. The war ended that, left Pa busted. Once this place bustled four nights a week. Now. . . .

Well, it's like Pa used to tell us: the only sure bets in this country are wind and dust. Which is all you'll find now. That, and crumbling ruins. And the dead.

You're 1,051 miles from Fort Smith, 460 1/2 from Fort Yuma. And 6 inches to Perdition. Pa always said that, too.

Pa—he was born Wallace Conner Munro, but most folks called him Conner, or Mr. Munro—used to tell us lots of things. He even said, fairly often, that a Scot from Boone County, Missouri, by way of South Carolina and Mississippi, could depend on his sons. Julian proved him wrong.

Reckon I did, too.

According to the family Bible, my name is Innis Smith Munro, but folks have always called me Smith, which came from Ma, Ainsley Smith Munro. She died three days after I was born, but Pa never blamed me for her passing. Nor did Julian, 11 years my senior. I've heard stories about fathers and siblings hating the child whose birth led to the mother's death, but that was never the case with us Munros. No, that hatred burned itself into our blood a dozen years after Ma was called to Glory.

Pa often said Ma would have thought of me as God's blessing, what with, between Julian and me, there being three stillborns and two girls who never lived more than a month. Every once in a while, Pa'd even call me a blessing.

Blessing.

Or maybe, like Tori Velásquez called this place, a curse.

The diary tells the story. I'm leaving it behind for whoever happens across it. In this accursed place, though, I would not tarry. Not that there's anything to keep anybody here.

Smith Munro

November 23, 1860

Friday. Eastbound brought this leather-bound diary, a birthday present from Julian. It's a week late, but that's all right. Julian's been busy, and Pa was glad to get a letter. I'm too tired to really write anything, though. Not even sure what I'm supposed to write. Stage was 20 minutes late, passengers irritable, though not as prickish as Pa was with Marco Max, the jehu.

"Mr. Butterfield was always preaching that 'nothing on God's earth must stop the U.S. Mail,' but you always test God, sir," Pa thundered at him, "and Wells, Fargo, and Company, and especially me!"

To which Marco Max said he was too tuckered out to listen to Pa throw worser a conniption than his sainted mother used to throw back in Vermont.

Mighty tuckered out myself. Maybe I'll think of something later to write down.

November 24, 1860

Slumgullion for breakfast, then work. Pa read Julian's letter again. Wish my brother had told me what a boy's supposed to write in a diary. A big Tobiano kicked Benjamin Jakes, that reprobate of a hand Superintendent Giles Hawley saddled us with, in the leg. The sorry cuss swore he'd kill that jenny as soon as he could walk again, but then Pa practically nailed his hide to the wall. Told Jakes he'd do no such thing, that he—Pa, I mean—had been breeding mules for nigh 20 years and Sweet Ainsley's the first Tobiano he ever seen.

She is a pretty mule, too. White legs, brown face with a snip, almost perfect brown ovals on her flanks, and mane and tail of two colors. Must be a tad taller than 16 hands. Only one like her that I've ever seen, but I ain't but 12. I like my mule, Ivanhoe, better, even if he is smaller and only a sorrel. But he's mine. Sweet Ainsley, she's Julian's.

"Sweet!" Jakes fired back at Pa, sweat from pain peppering his face. "Think that mule's sweet? It nigh broke my leg. I don't think I can walk."

"That figures." Pa didn't have much use for Jakes, lazy as a cur, always finding a way to get out of chores. Wouldn't surprise me if Jakes walked behind Sweet Ainsley apurpose.

"Smith!" the old man called out to me, practically begging. "Can you help this ol' hand to his bunk? My britches is 'bout to bust." He was rubbing his leg, which had swole up something fierce. Maybe it was busted after all.

"Smith's got work to do," Pa said flatly. He had disappeared into the stone-walled stable.

"Well . . . but. . . ." Ben Jakes almost sobbed. "How can I get to my bunk, Mr. Munro? I be bad hurt."

"Crawl," Pa told him.

November 25, 1860

Slumgullion for breakfast again. Pa watered it down even more so it'll last longer. Mighty sick of that poor-tasting stew, but it'll be the same for dinner and

supper, if we get supper. Westbound's due at 8:30 tonight. It's Sunday, but there ain't no Sabbath for the
Overland Mail Company, although Pa, as has been
his habit long as I can recollect, prayed and made
me recite a verse before breakfast.

" 'Jesus wept,' " I said. "John 11. Verse 35."

Pa's dark eyes bore through me. Julian used to
do that fairly often because it's the shortest passage in
the Bible. Sometimes Pa'd let him get away with it.
Other times, he'd threaten a whipping with his razor
strop. Wasn't sure what he was going to do to me this
morn, especially with them eyes so cold, but he finally looked at his plate, and told me: "Pass the stew."

Will write more if I get time.

November 26, 1860

Didn't get time last night to write no more. Stage was
on time, early in fact, but had to work harder because
Ben Jakes remained off his feet. Fact is, that leg of his
is black and blue as tarnation, still pretty swole up.
Eastbound should be back around midnight, if it's
on time, and Ben Jakes won't be no help. Seldom is.
Still, Pa's been in a good mood. So I asked him what
I was supposed to write in this here diary that Julian
give me.

"What do you want to write?" he asked me.

"I don't know."

"What have you been writing?"

I shrugged. "Just that Sweet Ainsley kicked Ben
Jakes. . . ."

"Mr. Jakes. He's your elder, Smith, worthless piece
of Texas trash that he is, you still call him Mr."

"Mr. Jakes. Just that he got kicked in his leg."

"That's good. You should have written that Sweet Ainsley had kicked him in his head. That would have been better."

I stared. Started to say—"But he wasn't kicked in the head."—only then Pa must have seen the look on my face, and he just laughed, laughed real hard, knocked the hat off my head, and tousled my hair. He ain't done that but once or twice since we left Boone County, Missouri.

"Your mother kept a journal," Pa said at last, and his face warmed the way it always did when he started talking about Ma. Warm, but sad. If you can picture that. Maybe you got to see it. I ain't the writer like Mr. Scott or Mr. Dickens.

"Ainsley must have filled ten of those books, maybe more. I never saw the use, but it's good practice for a boy your age. Not much book-learning to be had out here."

"Did you ever look at what Ma wrote?"

He shook his head. "Oh, she'd read a passage to me now and again. And when we left Port Gibson, we somehow lost one of her diaries, and she pitched a fit over that. Feared somebody would read it. 'Isn't that what it's for?' I asked her, and, by grab, that stirred her up like a hornet. 'No, Conner Munro, it most certainly is not!' she informed me. 'A diary is for the person writing in it. To record her innermost thoughts. Her wishes. Her hopes. Her dreams. . . .'"

Pa stopped. All of a sudden, he just stared at his boots. I started to say something, only decided against it. I'm only 12, but I ain't stupid. At last, Pa looked up, real quickly, then stood and turned away. "I guess," he said as he walked outside, "that's what you write. Whatever you want to, really. What you think. What you want."

"Like talking to God?" I asked.
"Maybe. I wouldn't really know."

Same day, 11 o'clock   •

Nighttime. Change of teams is in the stable, ready to go. That's how Mr. Butterfield told us to operate back when he run this show, and how Wells, Fargo, & Company still wants it run. We harness the mules together in the stable, then when the stage arrives, while the jehu and conductor are helping unhitch the wore-out team, we lead the fresh mules, already hitched together, to the Celerity coach. That's so a mule don't bolt away and cause a delay. The Overland don't like delays.

Pa don't neither.

I bet most boys my age ain't drinking coffee at eleven in the evening, but the Eastbounds don't get here till midnight—if they're on time—and I have to lend a hand, even if I don't draw no wages. But I'm with Pa. That's good enough for me.

Still not sure what all to write. Wish I had Ma's diaries to look at, but they ain't here. I asked Pa about them, but he just shook his head. Said he left them in Missouri with all of Ma's other things.

That ain't the truth, though. Julian told me. He's older, you see, eleven years older than me, so, once, right before he went off to West Point, he told me that right after Ma got called to Glory, when they wasn't sure I'd live much longer my ownself, that Julian woke up one night—probably as quiet as this one, least, that's how I picture it—and he got out of bed. Aunt Bertha, the midwife who had been tending to me since Ma's passing, was asleep, too. So was me. Only Pa and Julian was awake. My brother looked outside, and he seen a big fire, seen Pa. He said Pa was crying, but I don't believe that, not for a second. Must have been smoke in Pa's eyes is all. Anyway, Julian told me Pa was burning all of Ma's dresses and things. Julian couldn't never figure out why. Said he didn't dare ask. Don't blame him.

Reckon Pa burned her diaries that night, too.

November 27, 1860

Reading part of *The Three Musketeers* by Alexandre Dumas after we got the Westbound stage off—no delays, no problems, talked a bit to a boy from Memphis, said he was 13, going with his stepmother to join his pa at his spread in California east of Fountain Spring—it occurred to me that I ought to put some history in this diary.

Pa runs the Overland Mail Company station at Soldier's Farewell in New Mexico Territory, or, as a passel of folks have labeled this southern strip of desert, Arizona Territory. Some folks don't call it Soldier's Farewell, but *Los Penasquitos*, but don't ask me what that means. Not sure I even can say it right. One time, I heard Bartolomé talking to Alyvia Velásquez, and Bartolomé, sweeping his hands at the surroundings, called it, *El Lugar Que El Diablo Posee*. I asked them both what they was talking about, because I know *diablo* means devil and that pricked my interest a mite, but they just pretended not to savvy nothing I said.

This is what they call a timetable stop on Division

IV, running from Franklin, Texas—which many folks are starting to call El Paso—all the way to Tucson, where Superintendent Hawley has his headquarters.

Time's important everywhere on the Overland, and real important at a timetable stop. First thing Pa bought, before we left Missouri, was a fancy American Watch Company key-winder that must have set him back a right smart of money. Solid gold, and that pocket watch keeps time right near perfect, though Pa can guess the time almost as good just by looking at the stars or sun.

This is hard country. And lonely. Full of Apache Indians, though they have let the stagecoaches and stations alone, excepting when they want to steal mules. That's why Pa, when he was in San Antonio, stopped by the H.D. Norton & Brothers store and paid cash money—which is all the Norton boys would take—for a pile of those newfangled Colt revolving pistols and some other weapons. I ain't got to shoot one yet.

Our nearest neighbors would be other Overland employees at Barney's Station 19 miles west of here, or Ojo de la Vaca 14 miles to the east, over toward Cooke's Spring, where there's another station. We're a supper stop for the Westbound stagecoaches (Sundays and Wednesdays), but just change teams quick as we can on the Eastbounds (Tuesdays and Fridays). Emmett Mills works at Cooke's. Him and Julian got to be pretty good pals during the short time they knowed each other. Emmett's 19, I think.

We work here with Mr. Benjamin Jakes—I've already wrote about him—and a red-bearded guy named Fletcher. Once, when Fletcher first started working for Pa, I made the mistake of asking him what his full name was, and he just spit out tobacco juice, and answered: "Fletcher's all there is."

I was only 9 at the time, and I barked back at him to quit funning me, to tell me his full name, and that's when Pa grabbed my collar, jerked me into the stable we was building, and give me a lesson in manners. "You don't ask a man his name, Smith," he told me. "You don't ask him where he came from. If he wants, he'll tell you. If he says his name is Fletcher, his name is Fletcher, and if that's all there is, that's all there is. Mr. Fletcher."

Fletcher's all right. He don't say much, and I do call him Mr. Sometimes I pretend that's his first name.

We also have a Mexican named Bartolomé, who I wrote about briefly before, and he's a good hand with mules, which is practically all we run on this part of the Overland. Even Pa says Bartolomé—he ain't much older than me, so I don't have to call him Mr. or *señor*—is one of the best hands with mules he has ever seen, and that's mighty high praise, coming from Pa.

The only other neighbors we have, who ain't drawing time from the Overland, is the Velásquez family. They live on what's known as Walnut Creek, due northeast of here under the shade of Cow Springs Mountain. That's a joke. There ain't no walnut trees on that creek, 'cause it ain't much of a creek, nor have I ever seen a cow there, and that mountain sure don't throw out much shade. I'm not sure it's even bigger than Soldier's Farewell Hill.

In fact, there ain't a whole lot of shade nowhere in this country. About the tallest things that grow are these yucca cactus plants, although there's some nice cottonwoods over at Cow Springs. But here it's just the yuccas and some brush and a ton of dust.

I like the Velásquez family. They feed us real good when we visit, or they come see us. They make this flat bread called a *tortilla*, which I'd never had before I come to New Mexico, and beans—they call them *frijoles*—seasoned with chile peppers. Never ate nothing like that in Boone County, but those *frijoles* are something good. Good and hot. And the *tortillas* are tastier than the crackers or cornbread Pa serves passengers at the station. At least the *tortillas* ain't got worms in them, which is more than I can say about those crackers. And they ain't stale. Pa'll serve the cornbread till it's harder than one of them stones in the stable. Once, I heard Marco Max tell Pa he'd pinch the braided hair off a large cent coin. Not sure what that meant, but Pa just snorted, and Little Terry got a good chuckle out of it. Little Terry rides as messenger, or guard, on most of Marco Max's runs. His brother, Big Terry, and a fellow called Donnie Oh are the other regular jehu and messenger.

I think Julian's always been sweet on Alyvia, the oldest Velásquez daughter, the one who was talking to Bartolomé in Spanish that time I just wrote about. The other girl is Tori—that's short for Victoria—she can be a nuisance, being maybe a year older than me, but sometimes I'll dance with her when we have a fandango or something because Tori and Alyvia— and *Señora* Dolores, of course, their ma—are the only females in this part of the country. Their father's name is Alejondro. Pa says *Señor* Velásquez knows this territory better than anybody, and *Señor* Vee, which is what most of us call him, helped us build this place when we first got here, a little more than two years ago.

I'll write about how a Missouri boy came to Southern New Mexico Territory next chance I get. Pa's calling, and Pa ain't one to let me bide a minute more'n I have to.

More later.

Same day, 3 o'clock

My name is Innis Smith Munro. I wouldn't write that if this diary was just for me, but Ben Jakes, when I was bringing him his dinner, he said he'd heard I was writing in a diary, and then he went on to tell me that was a good thing, so my grandsons would know what life was like when I was a boy.

Ain't got much use for Ben Jakes—Mr. Ben Jakes, I mean—but what he told me sure got me to thinking. Of course, when I asked him if he kept a diary, he just snorted and said he didn't read nor write but heard about what other folks done. I also thought about Pa, if he had burned all those diaries Ma kept along with her clothes and such, how he might have robbed her grandchildren—and me and Julian, even—of knowing what she had seen and done and heard when she was growing up. Even after she had grown up. Besides, I already wrote before that I'd tell how a Missouri boy come to Soldier's Farewell. So here it is:

I, Innis Smith Munro, was born on November 13, 1848, at our farm in Boone County, Missouri. My brother, Julian, he was born in Camden, South Carolina, on March 12, 1837. I'm copying this here stuff from the Bible, which Pa keeps on the table in our house, which is only a 12×14 stone shack next to a 70×40 foot stable with stone walls 10 feet high. The mules live better than folks working at Soldier's Farewell, but, I reckon, they're probably more important in this desert.

Ainsley Abigail Smith was born in Camden, South Carolina, on July 16, 1818. Ma died on November 16, 1848, in Boone County, Missouri. Pa was born in 1816. No date. No town given. He married Ma on April 2, 1835, in Camden. There's nothing about my grandpas and grandmas, but there is a sentiment:

> To Conner and Miss Ainsley,
>   "Who can find a virtuous woman? for her price
> is far above rubies."
> > All my best on this blessed occasion,
> > > Wade Hampton III

I've heard Pa mention Wade Hampton before. He and Pa used to go bear hunting in Mississippi, where Wade Hampton had a plantation. He also had a bunch of land and slaves in South Carolina. Pa never owned no slaves. I'm not sure if he believes in what I heard some passengers call "the South's peculiar institution"—but bear hunting with Wade Hampton, that's how Pa discovered Mississippi, which is where the Munros moved to in 1842. The last I'd heard about Wade Hampton, he had been elected to the United States Senate. Reckon Pa hunted bear with a right famous fellow.

Ma, Pa, and Julian lived in Port Gibson, and that's where Pa joined the Mississippi Rifles about the time the war broke out with Mexico. Pa's still got the rifled musket he carried in that war. They call it a Mississippi Rifle. Pa says he ain't never had anything that shot so true. He says when I get a tad bigger, he'll let me shoot it, but, right now, all I can shoot is an Allen & Thurber Pepperbox, a little .31-caliber pistol he bought in the Nortons' store in San Antonio when he bought all those Colt pistols and rifles. Pa taught me how to shoot and load the Pepperbox, in case we get attacked by Indians or something.

It was with the Mississippi Rifles—Pa said the official name was the 155th Infantry Regiment but everybody called them the Mississippi Rifles, and that's about all he's ever spoke about that war—where he served under Colonel Jefferson Davis, who later became Secretary of War and is now also in the United States Senate. Pa knew some really important folks, didn't he?

It was in the war, at a place called Buena Vista, that Pa got bad hurt. Never talks about it, though, and I've learned it's best not to ask him, even though I'd sure like to hear all about that gore and glory. He come back to Port Gibson, and moved the family to Boone County, Missouri, and that's where he started raising mules. Which is where I was born. He often says all his mules was born in Missouri.

One time he said that I reminded him that Julian was born in Camden, and he let out a real belly laugh at that one, then admitted he had to correct himself. "I had one mule born in South Carolina, the rest"—and he'd knocked my hat off—"were sired in Boone County."

Mr. John Butterfield called Pa the best mule man in Missouri, but Pa said, as he'll often tells folks—"It takes an ass to breed a mule."—but Mr. Butterfield, being a pious fellow, didn't laugh at the joke. Pa went on to say, serious-minded, that, no, there was lots of good mule breeders in Central Missouri, and he allowed how David Hickman and Nathaniel Leonard, not to mention Doc Rollins, were some of the greatest jack-stock men you'll ever find. He also said

Eli Bass, just down the pike over toward Ashland, was better than Pa'd ever hope to be.

But Mr. John Butterfield hired Pa anyway.

By then, you see, Julian got an appointment to the U.S. Military Academy at West Point, New York. That sure made Pa and me proud. Didn't hurt that Pa knowed Jefferson Davis and Wade Hampton, Mr. Davis being in the U.S. Senate again and Mr. Hampton at that time serving in the South Carolina General Assembly. So in 1854, Julian set off for West Point. He said he'd be a "plebe"—whatever that is. By the time he graduated, 15th in a class of 27, in 1858, me and Pa had settled in New Mexico Territory.

More chores. Will finish later.

Same day, half past 8 o'clock

Pa won't like it none if he found out I was still writing in this diary and not sleeping—Westbound stage comes in tomorrow night, and Ben Jakes still ain't walking—but Pa and Fletcher shared a mite of corn whiskey after supper, and he's snoring on his bed.

I was 8 years old when Congress approved this mail contract to Mr. Butterfield and his associates. Congress agreed to pay $600,000—by jingo, that be a right smart of money—and Mr. Butterfield had a lot of work to do. Stagecoaches carrying mail, and some passengers, would leave twice a week from Missouri and California, and those stagecoaches had to get there in 25 days or less. That's 2,800 miles, meaning the stages would be running day and night.

I remember Pa telling how Mr. Butterfield first explained everything to him. I wasn't there. Pa had taken a matched set of buckskin mules—buckskins are fairly uncommon, too—to some place in New York, where he had sold the pair to this rich man, then gone to visit Julian at West Point.

"We shall put stations at intervals of 20 miles or so. Quick stops, but also a stop for breakfast and supper, but those will be no more than 40 minutes."

"You'll kill your driver," Pa told him.

"The jehu will go only 60 miles, the conductor no more than 120."

Pa still had his doubts. "Can't be done, sir."

"Can be done, sir," Mr. Butterfield said. "And will be done, by Jehovah. I've heard about your work with mules, seen your mules, and I have been told mules, not horses, are much better suited for the Western territories."

"That's true. They're sure-footed. Strong. Reliable."

"And Jesus Christ rode a mule."

"Wasn't one of mine." Pa had grinned. He said Mr. Butterfield didn't find much humor in the remark.

They haggled some, then Pa come back to Boone County, telling Mr. Butterfield to have his man look him up, and he'd sell him some mules. Mr. Butterfield didn't waste no time.

I reckon Pa had no notion of actually leaving Boone County till the Overland Mail Company man came to buy some mules. Lots of mules. They got to talking, and Pa glanced over at the little fence around Ma's grave, and suddenly started hounding the Overland man with questions about the route and what all it was going to take to get this business going.

"250 stagecoaches," the man had said, "1,800 horses and mules."

"And men?"

"1,200. Superintendents, guards, blacksmiths, clerks, drivers, stationmasters."

"All them positions filled?" Pa had asked.

November 28, 1860

The Velásquez family come over after breakfast. I wasn't paying no mind, reading some more of Mr. Dumas, when Tori snuck up from behind and yanked my hair. It's pretty long. Pa ain't got around to cutting it lately.

I turned around—that smarts, you know—and almost cut loose with a string of oaths anybody who has worked with mules has heard plenty of times.

"What are you doing?" I yelled at Tori, and then her ma started firing out some words in Spanish that I couldn't keep up with, and Tori looked down, muttering—"Sí, sí."—and lifted her eyes, her head still bowed, and said: "*Lo siento*, Innis Smith Munro."

I didn't say nothing, just glared at her. Tori's 13, but sometimes she acts like she's 3. She was wearing a colorful dress. Usually I see her in muslin and sandals, and her hair had been washed. I could smell the yucca soap she'd used. Yucca's a cactus that grows in these parts. I don't know how they make soap out of it. Pa uses lye soap. Makes me use it too, when I get around to taking a bath. Lye soap don't smell good, but it'll clean you down to your bones if you ain't careful.

Señor Vee checked in on Ben Jakes, and reported to Pa that the swelling was starting to go down, that he didn't think nothing was broke, and that Mr. Jakes would probably be up and around in a day or two.

"If not," *Señor* Vee said, "you should send him along his way."

"I should do that anyway," Pa said. He wouldn't, though. Not many folks wanted to work for the Overland in this here wasteland, and Mr. Jakes done some work, sometimes.

Then *Señora* Dolores brought out victuals she had brung us for dinner. "Roast lamb and fried potatoes," Tori told me, and we started setting up our table outside. Even Ben Jakes hobbled out of the little bunkhouse inside the stables, and we had us a regular feast.

"Have you heard from. . . ." Alyvia—she's 16, I'm guessing—looked kind of sheepish. "*Señor* Julian?"

Pa and *Señor* Vee exchanged looks, and then Pa smiled and told me to fetch the letter Julian had wrote. He read it aloud. Just now, I pulled that letter out from the old *Graham's Magazine* somebody left behind, which is where Pa keeps all of Julian's letters, and that ambrotype of him in his cadet uniform that he brung Pa. I'm copying down Julian's letter. It ain't much. Julian never wrote long letters, but he's busy.

15 November 1860
Pa:

I take pencil in hand to let you know that I am in good health and wish the same for you and Smith. Looks like I've forgotten Smith's birthday again, but at least I'm not too late, so I'm sending this diary. He needs to practice his letters and grammar. Tell him I don't expect to find this diary in the privy next time I'm out there. [Pa mumbled through that part when he read it aloud to the

Velásquez family, but still blushed a mite.] *Tell him to write.*

We're finally back at Fort Tejon after spending months chasing Paiutes on our "punitive expedition" under command of Captain James H. Carleton for what happened at Bitter Springs on the Salt Lake Trail. I'm not sure Paiutes murdered those two white men there. I think they might have been killed by white men, but second lieutenants do not question their orders. Heard from George Bascom. You remember him? We were in the same class at the Academy, though he's older than me. We got a pass together when you came to West Point that time after selling that rich hotel man those buckskin mules. George is stationed at Fort Buchanan with the 7th Infantry. I wrote him that I've finally seen the elephant. It got hot, but, as I've said, I am unscathed, though burned a dark brown by the sun. If you think Soldier's Farewell is brutal, you should spend months in the saddle in the Mojave Desert fighting Paiutes.

I'm sure you've heard the talk of war back East. All the officers are discussing it at Fort Tejon.

I have to close for now. Wish you and the little kid well. Tell him Happy Birthday from me.

Your loving son,
Julian Munro
2nd Lieutenant
1st U.S. Dragoons
Fort Tejon, California

I'd heard Pa read that letter twice, but now he didn't sound so excited, and I realized it wasn't that happy a note. Maybe it was only then that I first heard, I mean understood, most of the words.

"What does 'see the elephant' mean?" I asked.

"He's been in battle."

"Really?" Now that excited me.

"I will thank the Blessed Virgin that he is safe," *Señora* Dolores said.

Pa told her: *"Gracias."*

"Boy's right about the talk of war," Ben Jakes said as he filled his mouth with lamb and potatoes. "That's all I been hearin', and I reckon I'll be makin' my way to Texas to fit with 'er if the North keeps provokin' us."

"You do that," Pa whispered, so low I think I was the only one who heard him, me being closest to him.

"What war would that be?" I asked. "With the Paiutes? The Apaches?"

I don't know rightly what a Paiute is, but I know all about Apaches. As I've wrote before, we live right smack dab in Apache country, and a few of them have taken a fancy to our mules. Either Pa, Bartolomé, Fletcher, or Ben Jakes will be on guard duty. I've told Pa I could stand a turn, but he ain't yet give me a chance.

"No," Pa answered.

I was about to ask him—"Well, who then?", getting a mite irritable, I was—but *Señora* Dolores blurted out that this was to be a happy celebration, and that she had not been informed that I had a birthday recently, so she told us all to forget any gloom, that Lieutenant Julian remained safe and healthy, that it was a beautiful day in November, and we, too, had our health.

So we ate up. Except Pa. Reckon he was off his feet some, but he still sat at the table with us, sipping coffee, pretending to, anyhow, and smiling, only I didn't see much enjoyment behind his eyes.

Same day, quarter past 9 o'clock

Westbound stage came and went. I'd hoped *Señor* Vee would stay and help with changing teams, but the Velásquezes can be peculiar folks, being Mexicans, I reckon, and *Señora* Dolores wouldn't hear of being here after dark. They sometimes act like this place is full of haunts and such, but I never seen no ghost.

Still, we fed the Westbound passengers our leftovers, so those travelers got more for their dollar than most folks get.

I forgot to finish my story about how we all got here.

Once Pa and the Overland man started talking about the positions, the Overland man told Pa to get to Tipton when he got a chance and to talk to this fellow named Lauer, that he was the man to see about hiring as the fellow at our house was just buying mules.

Well, next thing I knowed, we had sold most of our mules and breeding stock to Eli Bass—keeping some of our best animals—and was bound for New Mexico Territory. That was in the spring of 1858. Pa and me met up with Superintendent Hawley in Franklin, Texas, where they hired some men, and we headed west. We crossed the ferry over the Río Grande north of Fort Fillmore, and followed the old Fort Webster Road—which wasn't that old, really— through the pass near Cooke's Spring, and lighted at Soldier's Farewell.

"How'd this place get its name?" I asked Pa.

Pa just stared. We'd never seen no country like this, that's certain sure, and never felt a sun as hot as this. That's saying something, because I'd sweated out a ton of water back in Missouri.

"It's the end of the earth," Pa said.

That's been a joke betwixt me and Pa. I'll ask him how this place come to be called Soldier's Farewell, and he'll think of some answer. I'm right certain he knows. What I don't know is if he's ever give me the truthful answer, but I suspect he's just telling me nothing but falsehoods. It's a game. Julian and I have a game, too.

We'll look at the clouds, and imagine they're something other than clouds. Once, I pointed to our cabin in Missouri. And Julian spotted a dun mule. Another time, he pointed to what he said was North Barracks, but I couldn't tell what he meant. Don't know a thing about North Barracks.

Julian's only been here once. That was after he was graduated from the Academy. He come here waiting for his orders, which he got a short while later. So he had a hand in building this place, and changing teams and feeding folks and taking a turn standing watch so Apaches didn't run off our mules. Hear tell they eat mules. They better not eat Sweet Ainsley, or, worser yet, my mule Ivanhoe. We didn't finish the station and stable till that November. By then, Julian was off to California as an officer in the dragoons.

The first stagecoaches started coming in mid-September of '58 when there wasn't nothing up yet but a tent. It was something hectic when the wagons would arrive afore we got everything built. Ain't slowed down since.

November 30, 1860

Didn't have a chance to write nothing yesterday or this morning. Eastbound came through on time. Wind's blowing something fierce, and you should see the clouds over the mountains to the west. Wish Julian was here. I'd tell him I see the face of Poseidon, the darkest part of those clouds being the Greek god's beard. Bitter cold. You wouldn't think how cold the desert gets, but that wind makes it unbearable. Maybe it'll rain.

December 1, 1860

Ben Jakes is up and around, complaining though. I sure miss the Velásquez crew. Even Tori. Well, mostly I miss the grub they brung. We're back to jerked beef, wormy crackers, maybe bacon, but mostly slumgullion stew.

December 2, 1860

The Westbound came through tonight, and there was a lot of talk at the supper table. I want to think about it, make sure I remember everything right, before I write it all down in this book.

It's Sunday. For my breakfast Bible verse, I surprised Pa. I read Matthew 7:24, where Jesus says: "Therefore whosoever heareth these sayings of mine, and doeth them, I will liken him unto a wise man, which built his house upon a rock."

Lot of rocks here.

December 3, 1860

Reread all that I've wrote so far. Still trying to think about the conversation from the previous day before I put it down.

They say there's almost no water along the Overland Trail between Texas and Tucson. The spring at Soldier's Farewell isn't far, in a ravine northeast of here. Before the dragoons came through in '56, travelers camped north of the peak near Hawk Springs. Anyway, when we got here, my job was to dam up the spring we use now. I bet I hauled two tons of rocks, putting calluses on calluses on my hands. But when Pa and Superintendent Hawley looked at my work, they said I was worth twice the wages I was drawing. They was funning. I ain't drawing no wages.

Then Pa, he knocked the hat off my head, pulled me close to him, and said to Mr. Hawley: "Smith's a blessing, Giles."

To which Mr. Hawley said: "I warrant he is. You done fine work, son."

To me, that was better than any wages from the Overland Mail Company.

Same day, half past 4 o'clock

Fire's going in our house. Bitter cold. Wind hasn't slacked a whit. Nary a drop of rain.

Let me describe my home. The door to the house, and gate to the big stables, face southwest. Fireplace is in the north corner, but I think it draws most of the heat from it. Usually that ain't so bad, because most days it gets blistering hot. Inside the stable, next to the gate, there's a 10×12 room, and that's where the other men live. The wall is nothing but rock slab, but it stands 10 feet high. Pa yelled at me twice when we was building it, telling me not to climb on that thing, that I'd break my neck, and usually Pa don't have to tell me a thing more than once, but that wall, when it was just being built, that was hard for a boy to resist. So Pa had to yell at me again a few days later.

He didn't have to tell me no more. By jingo, I could hardly sit down for a week after the second time.

If there ain't no dust storm, you can see the beginnings of the Burro Mountains. When the Westbound leaves, that's where it's heading, first to Barney's Station. But the stage don't go into the real mountains. *Señor* Vee says that's some real spectacular country.

The nearest mountains are called the Langfords, but, if you ask me, they don't amount to much. Rough country. Not much but creosote and saltbrush here, and them yuccas I've wrote some about, though higher up, *Señor* Vee says, you'll find an oak and some mountain mahogany.

It was from the Big Burros that Pa and *Señor* Vee traveled when we was building the station to fetch a flagstaff. They brung back a Ponderosa pine they'd chopped down, and went to work on it, turning it into a flagpole that got erected right outside the bunkhouse in the stable.

Mr. Butterfield had said Overland stations were part of the U.S. Mail, and thus should be flying the American flag. Pa agreed, but the first stage hadn't run yet, so when he and *Señor* Vee put up that flagstaff and unfurled the colors, it wasn't to please Mr. Butterfield or Superintendent Hawley. No, that was for Julian.

Don't know where that flag come from. Sure is a ragged-looking thing.

The flag was flying two days before Lieutenant Julian Munro come home. That was July 23, 1858.

December 4, 1860

Tuesday. The Eastbound came through at half past midnight, 30 minutes late. Wind still howling.

December 5, 1860

Thinking of Julian, I'll get back to my story about when he first came here.

I got to raise the flag this morning. Usually Pa does it, but D.N. Barney, the director who runs the change station west of here, showed up for coffee and confidential business talk.

Back to Julian and two years ago:

We knowed he was coming, only wasn't sure when, and he just showed up that July morning with a couple of carpetbags and a high-stepping horse, looking like a real gentleman in that uniform, except for his excuse for a mustache, and proudly showing us his "sheepskin"—that's what he called the diploma that proved he was a graduate of the United States Military Academy. That and his ring.

Pa, well, I never seen him so proud. Figured he might up and bust. He told us that his grandma and grandpa were the first Munros to even learn how to read and write, and he never expected to see one of his own children go and get a real education, and serve all of our United States.

"I'll be in the dragoons," Julian said. "They'll send orders directly."

Well, Pa, he insisted we throw a *baile*. *Señor* Vee brung down his family, and *Señora* Dolores cooked and cooked, and, by jingo, I never seen such food. Emmett Mills come down from Cooke's. That's when he first met my brother, and Emmett and Julian took to each other like brothers. They was always off hunting, or racing. Kind of made Alyvia Velásquez jealous. Don't reckon I cared much for Emmett hogging my brother like that, neither.

That's when Pa presented Julian with his gift. You should have seen the look in my big brother's eyes when he first saw that jenny. Like I say, a big Tobiano like that ain't a mule one sees every day.

"The Army provides mounts, Pa," Julian had said, "and I do own a horse."

"Yeah, and I've seen that horse you paid hard money for, Jules," Pa had said with a snort. "But I'll keep her here for you. She'll get better treatment than with your dragoons."

"I'd appreciate that. What are your rates to stable her?"

"We can work something out. I hear the Army doesn't pay much more than John Butterfield."

"Sounds like you just want a reason for me to come back here."

Pa was staring off toward Mexico. He started to say something, yet didn't finish, then looked at Julian standing there in the wind, him having to hold that cap on his head with both hands.

"That's what I want," Pa said. "That's payment enough. You come back."

I didn't understand all of that. Not then. Not until maybe when Pa read that letter to the Velásquez family a few days back, and I realized that being a lieutenant in the 1st U.S. Dragoons might not all be glory. Pa had "seen the elephant" down in Mexico with the Mississippi Rifles, and he had almost gotten himself killed at Buena Vista. It struck him that Julian, his oldest son, my only brother, could right easily get killed out West.

Julian wasn't here long, and, like I wrote, he spent most of that time with Emmett Mills, though he'd sneak down to see Alyvia a time or two, probably more often than that. Finally the orders came, and we all had to say good bye. He was to proceed to Fort Tejon in California.

"That's just down the road," Pa said.

"Then y'all come visit," Julian told us. He looked off into the desert, suddenly grinned, and said: "I guess this is how this place earned its name. A soldier's farewell."

"Not farewell," Pa said. "This is just. . . ." He whispered something in Spanish.

"Till we meet again." Julian nodded.

We shook hands. I used to like it when Julian would kiss my cheek good bye, but finally I got too big for that stuff, and I liked it more when he'd shake my hand. Made me feel like a grown-up. That morning, I offered him my hand, waiting for that firm shake, but Julian knelt down and pulled me close to him, held me the longest time, and, thunderation, he up and kissed my cheek.

"Jules," I cried out, wiping his slobber off my face, "I'm way too big for that!"

"My apologies, sir," he said, and turned to Pa. They shook hands, and then Julian did the strangest thing. He pulled Pa close to him, and they embraced, and he hauled off and kissed Pa's cheek. You never seen Pa's face turn so red.

Julian had a horse, a muscular bay stallion—Pa didn't care much for him, though—which he'd saddled. And he swung up on top and tipped his cap at us.

"You ain't named that jenny Pa gave you," I told him.

"That's true," Julian said. "She'd feel lost without a name."

I was betting he'd name that mule Alyvia, but my big brother fooled me.

"Sweet Ainsley," he said.

Pa's face softened. "That's a fine name."

Then, Julian rode off.

Ain't seen him since.

December 8, 1860

It's been a few days since I've written. But I've heard more talk about the troubles back East, so now I think I can write about that supper-table conversation I overheard back on the 2nd. It went like this:

One of the passengers was a tall gent in a flat-crowned straw hat who hailed from Indiana. Name was Reagan. Said he had business in San Francisco. The other man, wearing spectacles that he was constantly wiping with a rag, come from Mississippi. I don't know where he was bound to or what his name was, and, like Pa had learned me, I knowed better than ask no questions. Other passengers kept quiet, just wolfing down their slumgullion or slurping coffee.

I wasn't paying attention to what those two gents was saying, just filling coffee cups, running the soles off my boots, until the Mississippi man slammed his fist on the table, and shot up real quick.

"By thunder, sir!" he roared, "I voted for John C. Breckinridge, and you shall withdraw your comment, or we shall meet on the field of honor. Right here. Right now." The man had dropped both his spectacles and his dirty handkerchief and had gripped the handle of a big Bowie, looked more like a saber than a knife, belted across his waist.

That room turned real quiet. I forgot all about how heavy that coffee pot was I kept holding.

"I believe, sir," Mr. Reagan said, "that if you are challenging me to a duel, it is customary for me to choose weapons. So you might let go of that toothpick." I hadn't noticed, don't reckon nobody had, but that Indiana man had been eating with his right hand, keeping his left underneath the rough-hewn table, but now he brought up his left hand, which was holding a big-bore boot pistol, aimed at the Mississippian's belly.

That's when I dropped the coffee pot. Nobody seemed to notice, and I just froze there, letting the hot tar Pa brewed soak into the dirt floor.

"You. . . ." The Mississippi man glared.

Mr. Reagan cocked the single-shot pistol, and the Southerner jerked his hand off that knife handle like it was hotter than the coffee I'd just spilt. The Indiana gent didn't lower the cocked .50-caliber, not yet, nohow.

"All I said, sir," Reagan said, "was that the recent election was a godsend for the states, both North and South."

The Mississippi man had to bite back whatever he was thinking about telling Mr. Reagan.

"Senator Douglas is a good man, but if you had heard one of the debates with President Lincoln a couple of years ago, as I had the honor of doing when, by fate, business took me to Galesburg, you would have had no doubt as to which man is the better candidate. But that Kentucky blow-hard, Breckinridge, is an atrocity, sir, and I will not withdraw what I said, respectfully." Slowly he lowered the hammer on the copper percussion cap, but didn't put away the pistol. "You have the floor, sir."

"You don't really know Senator Breckinridge," the Mississippi man said. "He's a good man, loyal, willing to serve his people. Not just Northern people, but *his* people."

"He never should have agreed to run, not on the terms you Southrons demanded. But you are correct. I do not know Senator Breckinridge. I know, however, what he stands for. Or, rather, what you fire-eaters stand for."

"You're a da- Abolitionist," the Mississippi man said. "Just like your Mr. Lincoln."

" 'Not an Abolitionist, hardly an anti-slavery man.' Those are the words from Wendell Phillips, an outspoken Abolitionist, about our new President. Nor am I. I am merely a humble Hoosier who fought in the war against Mexico, and who cherishes all about this nation. Mr. Phillips went on to say perhaps Lincoln is a 'pawn on the political chessboard.' I think he is far from that, but a great man, a great leader. I do not hold with slavery. But it's the South's institution, so let the South deal with it. Yet I will not see this blight of yours spread across the continent."

The Southern man tried to stand taller. "The South will deal with it, as we shall deal with you despots if you force our hand. Mayhap you already have. That farce of an election was just what we needed."

"You should remember Mr. Lincoln's words . . . 'A house divided against itself cannot stand.' "

"You Northerners have forced us into this. Remember that when the streets of Pennsylvania Avenue are 10 feet deep with blood, gore, and the mangled bodies of Northern dead. You shall see who wins your game of chess."

"Then it's your move, sir."

Well, I was sweating, and the Mississippi man started reaching for his knife, while the Hoosier gent again thumbed back the hammer on that cannon of a little pistol. That's when Pa walked in.

"If you're stumping, do it outside. This ain't Charleston. This ain't Washington City. And here's the law at Soldier's Farewell." Pa pointed at the coffee pot. "Both of you are paying extra for that."

One hand moved away from the Bowie knife, and the boot pistol finally returned to its home.

Pa's a big man. Powerful as a Missouri mule. One time, Marco Max said of him to me: "Your pa's the onliest man I know who can lift a Celerity wagon off the ground . . . while he's standing atop it."

Both the Indiana man and the Southerner fished out a coin from their vests, and dropped them on the table in front of their bowls.

"I'd put a muzzle on any political debates," Pa told them. "It's a long way to California. Now get out. Stage leaves in 5 minutes."

December 9, 1860

Abraham Lincoln got elected president of our nation back on Tuesday, November 6. I guess I should have knowed that before now, but I never had much interest in those kinds of things, not like I got in the stories of Mr. Dumas and Mr. Dickens and, especially, Mr. Scott. Stories, I like a whole lot. There's some good stories in the Bible, too.

Other than the Bible, we only own four books, not counting a couple of readers we brung from Missouri, along with two dictionaries—Noah Webster's American Dictionary of the English Language from 1852 and the Pronouncing Germany Dictionary, which Pa bought back in Missouri because there was so many Dutchies moving in that country and bartering for his mules, but we haven't had much need of such a book here at Soldier's Farewell. I've read the novels I don't know how many times. Julian, when he was passing through here two years ago, promised he'd send along some Shakespeare, but he ain't done it yet. But I can read *The Three Musketeers, Ivanhoe, The Adventures of Oliver Twist* and *The Yemassee* by William Gilmore Simms. Pa says Ma enjoyed that Simms fellow a lot, but I like Scott the best of all. And Pa makes me read the Bible. Says it's for Ma.

I'm not even sure who was President before him, but I think it must have been Andrew Jackson, because I've heard his name bandied around a lot. Anyway, from all I've heard recently, I'm not sure this President Lincoln is that popular. Mr. Reagan from Indiana, and the man with the glasses from Mississippi ain't the only passengers I've heard debating the elections, the prospects for war, the North, the South, Abolition and slavery.

The South is threatening to abolish the Union.
That's what dominated most of the talk at supper
tonight on the Westbound.

"If that happens, there will be war, sure enough,"
said a man in a silk hat.

"Won't last long," commented another, a tobacco
chewer who spit oftener than anyone I ever seen.
The talked civil, though, so I wasn't afraid that they
might slash or shoot one another.

December 10, 1860

Where should I stand on all this talk about war, about
the North and the South? Not even sure what I am. I
mean, my family hails from South Carolina, and
lived in Mississippi for a spell. That's South, and,
from what I've heard in passing, those two states
are the biggest talkers about quitting the Union, and
preaching war, the rights of the individual states,
things like that. I wonder what Senator Davis and
Senator Hampton are saying back in Washington.
Wonder where Pa stands in this thing.

I'm a Missourian. I guess I am. Was born there,
anyhow. But for the life of me, I can't figure out if
Missouri is for the North or for the South. Slavery's
a big part of the talk, but I hear more talk about the
rights of the states, and the necessity that the Union
survives, even if it costs lives. I saw a few slaves in
Missouri, but Pa never did own none, and he ain't
never talked about any rights, states or nothing.

It don't always even seem to be about the North and
the South. A while back, these two gents from Ohio,
which I'm right sure is in the North, was talking
about this coming war, and the guy from Columbus

was arguing one way, and the man from Cincinnati another. The Columbus fellow called the Cincinnati gent a "doughface"—which Marco Max explained to me later is what they call a Northern man who has sympathies for the South.

Big changes. Pa often says that change is one thing that a body has to realize is going to happen. And this family has been through plenty of changes, what with us moving first to Mississippi, then to Boone County, and finally the Territory. What with Ma dying like she done. What with Julian going off to West Point and now in California.

"Everything changes," Pa said, "except the wind and dust blowing."

Changes with the Overland Mail Company, too. Back in March of this year, John Butterfield had to quit the company he started. Seems he owed a passel of money to this Wells, Fargo, & Company, which is what's running the Overland now. That wasn't no real change, I warrant. After all, here at Soldier's Farewell, things seem about the same. I never considered Mr. Butterfield the boss of this operation. Land's sake, he ain't never been west of Fort Smith, Arkansas, from what I've heard, and I don't think Mr. Wells or Mr. Fargo runs things, neither. Nor Superintendent Hawley over in Tucson. At Soldier's Farewell, Pa's the boss.

Everybody knows it, too.

December 11, 1860

Rained today. Think it might be snowing in the mountains higher up north of here.

December 15, 1860

It finally happened. Fletcher said he seen it coming. Only I had no idea. Emmett Mills, who come by just to visit and bring some news to Pa from Cooke's Spring, he and Ben Jakes got into fisticuffs this afternoon. They was arguing about the war—like the war has already begun—and pretty soon they was trading blows. Emmett's a Union man. Ben Jakes is a Texican. North and South. Well, Ben Jakes threw the first punch, but that's about all he got to do because one thing I learned today is you never want to get Emmett Mills riled up. Beat the tar out of Mr. Jakes, he did. Might could have killed him if Pa hadn't stepped in, and sent Emmett a-sprawling. You also don't want Pa riled up.

December 16, 1860

Snowed. First time I've seen snow since Missouri, even if it was just a dusting. I finally got around to asking Pa about this war, and where we should stand if the fight come to us.

He didn't answer for a long time.

"Don't fret over that, Smith," he finally told me. "We're in New Mexico Territory, more than 1,000 miles from those fire-eaters. War, if there is a war, will not touch us."

But it already has.

That's what I wanted to tell Pa, thinking about that fellow from Mississippi and Mr. Reagan from Indiana. Closer than them two, just yesterday, it come to us, touched us, when Emmett and Ben Jakes had their row. But I just told Pa: "Yes, sir."

December 19, 1860

Been a trifle busy. Snow's all gone, but the wind ain't slowed down even a bit. Tonight, feeding the folks on the Westbound, this rich-looking gent from the California gold fields asked if we always seasoned our stew with dirt, instead of salt.

If he thought his supper was full of dirt, he should have sampled breakfast this morning.

Another man asked if it was possible somewhere along the Overland to have a fried egg. And that got me to thinking when was the last time I'd even seen an egg. Or even a chicken. By jingo, I don't reckon I've even spied nary a quail's nest to rob since we left the States.

Going to bed hungry, dreaming of something to eat other than slumgullion or bread that does its best to break your teeth.

December 20, 1860

Trouble. Bad trouble. Apaches run off about a dozen mules. Including Sweet Ainsley!

December 21, 1860

Eastbound come through. Pa ain't here. Went off yesterday to get the mules. No time to write.

December 22, 1860

No word from Pa.

December 23, 1860

Pa still ain't back. Hope he ain't dead. Praying he ain't dead. Give Marco Max a letter to leave at Fort Tejon for Julian, explaining that Pa's off chasing Apaches.

December 24, 1860

Snowing again. On Christmas Eve. Should be singing carols or reading the Bible or something. But reckon I'll write.

Back on Thursday morn, we discovered the missing mules, and Pa was inclined to stove in Ben Jakes's head with a singletree. Jakes—I ain't calling him Mr., not now, not after what he done—swore he wasn't asleep when he was supposed to be standing watch, but nobody believes him. Jakes is lucky the Apaches didn't slit his throat.

Well, we had enough mules for the Eastbound the next day, and I reckon the Missouri mules we stock on this part of the Overland is all tough enough to make it down the pike to the next station. Shucks, when the mail first started running back in '58, there wasn't no station betwixt Soldier's Farewell and Stein's. Them first stages had to go 42 miles west without water, but now there's Barney's Station.

Things could have been a lot worser. If them Indians had taken all of our livestock, we'd all be afoot. Nice of them to leave us some mules, and, especially, all of Pa's prime breeding stock.

We sent word east and west down the trail and over to *Señor* Vee, who come quick with a musket and a double-action Adams .36, and I hadn't never seen him with no pistol before. Wearing a brace of Colts

and carrying his Mississippi Rifle, Pa said he was
going after those thieves, and *Señor* Vee said he expected that, and that he was more than a fair hand at
following a trail, even a trail left by Apaches. I quickly
yelled that I'd be coming too, that no dirty Indian
was going to steal my brother's mule, but Pa wouldn't
let me come along.

Said I was too little.

I about to cried. That surely hurt my feelings, and
I was about to argue with Pa, but he wasn't in no
mood for arguing. Emmett Mills come along directly, said he'd be joining the party, and Mr. Barney
sent along a fellow named Cooper. Pa threw a saddle
on a big mule he calls Boss.

Reckon if Apaches was any judge of mule flesh
they would have taken Boss with them. Boss was
sired by a big old black Mammoth Jack, with a Percheron mare as the dam. Boss stands better than 16
hands tall and weighs about 1,400 pounds. Mule like
that could have fed a whole Apache *ranchería*.

That makes me sick. Thinking how them Indians
might have already eaten Sweet Ainsley.

Same day, after supper

Ain't sure of the time. Pa taken his watch with him.
Still ain't back yet. *Señora* Dolores come along this
evening with Alyvia and Tori, and even Tori was on
good behavior. I bet her ma warned her not to act
foolish or rotten what with all the stuff that has been
going on.

She brung along supper. Wasn't hungry. Still worried about Pa.

Pa up and left Fletcher in charge whilst he's gone. And right before he rode off, he pointed a big finger at Ben Jakes and said any mule that wasn't returned would be coming out of that scalawag's pay. And if Sweet Ainsley wasn't returned. . . .

Well, Pa didn't finish that threat. Don't reckon he had to.

Surprised Ben Jakes ain't run off yet.

Señora Dolores left after supper. Took the girls with her. I thought they might stay this time, what with Apaches in the area and all, but they didn't. Just don't like this place after dark. She wished me a fine Christmas, said she'd come back tomorrow, and told me not to worry about Pa or her husband.

I told her I wasn't worried at all. Pa and *Señor* Vee knowed how to take care of themselves.

Lying, of course. Is that a bigger sin to lie on Christmas Eve?

Hope Pa ain't dead.

December 25, 1860

Christmas. Eastbound come through almost three hours late. Pa would have raised Cain over that.

Bad worried.

December 26, 1860

Tomorrow it will be a week since Pa took off chasing the Apaches. A rider come through this afternoon, and when I seen him, I thought it might be Julian. But it was just some Mexican. Fletcher asked if he'd seen any sign of anything, but the Mexican said no, hadn't seen nobody hardly since he crossed the border on the Janos Road.

Warned him that Apaches had stolen some mules.

Fed him the last of the slumgullion, and didn't charge him nothing on account it was so near Christmas and he looked like he hadn't eaten since he'd left Janos.

December 27, 1860

Pa ain't back. Ain't none of us much a hand at cooking, and we're trying to figure out what to feed the Westbound when the stage comes through on Sunday. Not to mention what we can eat. Maybe *Señora* Dolores will bring us some chuck. Ain't seen her since Christmas.

Hope she ain't dead, neither.

December 28, 1860

Eastbound come through, late, with a wagon full of passengers. A fellow riding up top yelled down if we had any recent news about South Carolina. Something big must be going on back yonder, but we ain't heard nothing. Nothing from the States. More importantly, nothing from Pa or *Señor* Vee.

December 29, 1860

Pa's back! He's alive. PRAISE GOD!

December 30, 1860

Pa and I wrote us a letter to Julian, which we're sending on the Westbound when it comes tonight, telling him not to fret none from my previous letter, that Pa was alive, that everybody was alive, that he come back with Sweet Ainsley, who the Apaches didn't eat after all, even if they is partial to mule meat.

Well, that was some story Pa told us. I practically cried when I saw him, his face covered with beard and dirt and grime. He give me a big hug, shook Fletcher's hand, even didn't act like he wanted to give Ben Jakes a good thrashing. It was evening when he come in, just before dusk.

"What's for supper?" he asked after he got all the mules—they brung back all but two, no three. I forgot all about Boss, the mule Pa rode out on. "What's for supper?" he asked again.

Bartolomé, Fletcher, and me just stared at our feet.

Same day, 7 o'clock

Pa said *Señor* Vee is a mighty fine tracker. Not that they needed some famous scout to follow the trail the mules and Apaches had left. It looked like, Pa said, those Indians didn't count on being followed.

They must have figured we was all yellow.

Them Apaches sure don't know Pa. Well, they didn't. They sure do now.

The trail led east and a bit north, through this little forest of yucca, but not along the Overland, and for a while there Pa and *Señor* Vee was struck with this gut-wrenching fear, on account it looked like those Apaches was making a beeline for the Velásquez place, but right before they hit the creek, which is dry this time of year, and dry most times of the year, the Apaches drove the mules down past Little Grandmother Mountain.

That's mighty miserable country. Like most of what they call mountains down here, Little Grandmother ain't much of a hill, and Grandmother Mountain, southwest of the little one, don't rise a whole lot higher, and neither one's a real mountain, just what they call a collection of plugs and flows. Looks like a cone, both of them mountains. The wind kept blowing, and it a bitterly cold wind, too. Pa called it "a vengeful, Old Testament wind" when he was telling us the story, his eyes shining and him having a great time with his belly full off some of the mescal Mr. Fletcher had bought off some drummer a while back.

Not much for mules to graze on down there. About all that grows is creosote and tarbush, and nary a thimble of water to be had. They come upon a lava flow, and that's where they found the carcass of the first mule. Wasn't one of them we'd brung from Missouri, but a good brown jenny some other mule man had sold Mr. Butterfield.

The poor animal had broke a leg, so the Apaches had butchered her and had a veritable feast. The Indians had left some meat behind, and it hadn't quite spoiled yet, it being so cold and all, so *Señor* Vee cut off some meat, and they ate supper that night in that lava flow.

"First time I've ever had mule," Pa said. "Not bad to eat. Apaches are fair smart, I've learned."

By then, Pa was in his cups pretty fair.

Well, from that old lava flow, the trail pretty much dried up, and Pa said he didn't have an inkling how *Señor* Vee knowed where to go. But they followed him. It was then, while Pa was telling this story, that Bartolomé asked *Señor* Vee how he knew which way the Apaches was going when they wasn't leaving no trail.

"They left sign," he said real soft-like, grinning and pointing at his dark eyes. "You just have to be able to see it."

"You saw it, Alejondro," Pa told him. "Because we found some apples the next day and knew we were right behind those Apaches."

From there, the trail turned south and west, through some of the roughest draws a body's ever seen, and into the Cedar Mountains. That's another bad name. Makes me think the folks who give places in this territory names are the worst grafters this side of St. Louis. Cedars! You won't find a cedar in those mountains, not even many junipers.

What Pa and the men found was the Apaches.

"Those mountains are like a fort," Pa said. "Steep, mean cañons. I thought we'd be rubbed out, because that country is just prime for an ambush. We were out of the wind, though, cold as it was, I still found myself drenched with sweat. That's when I saw the savage."

"Chiricahua," *Señor* Vee said. *"Muy mal."*

The Apache, who said his name was Dasoda-hae, sat atop a big black pony, and he was a mean-looking Indian with a dark face peppered with scars, a dirty red bandanna tied around his head. Only wearing moccasins and some deerskin leggings, and this red calico shirt, faded to almost pink, and he come riding, old musket in his hands, barrel pointing skyward. Pa and the others stopped, and Emmett Mills started for his own six-shooter, but Pa told him to hold off.

"They'll kill us," Emmett said.

"They could have killed us a hour ago," Pa said. "This one has come to talk."

So they commenced to have a little parley, with the Apache talking in bits of Spanish and *Señor* Vee translating what he could for Pa. When they couldn't savvy none of the words, those two would just talk with their hands. Pa said he'd heard about signing with Indians before, but that was the first time he'd ever seen it done.

The Indian, Pa said, looked older than dirt. In his 60s, Pa said, and maybe even older than that. Big chief of the Bedonkohes. Speaking through *Señor* Vee's hands, Pa told the Apache they was supposed to be at peace, but the Apache said that peace had done been broken.

"Tell him who it was, Mr. Munro!" Emmett Mills pleaded with Pa during Pa's storytelling, but we all told Emmett to hush up, enraptured as we was with this report.

Seems like, the way the Apache put it, some miners from around Burchville—that's up in the Pinos Altos region way north of Soldier's Farewell—had attacked the Bedonkohe camp on the Río Mimbres. That wasn't the first time them miners had done that old Apache wrong. Some eight, nine, maybe ten years back, miners had tied that Apache to a tree and whipped him. And Apaches ain't a forgetting or forgiving breed of man.

This time, them miners had killed four of his people, and stolen better than a dozen women and children. So the Apaches was at war.

"Your war is with the miners in the Santa Rita Mountains," Pa told him. "Not the Overland Mail."

Now it was plain that the Apache and *Señor* Vee

had little use for one another, but the Chiricahua was an honorable man. That's what Pa said. Honorable. I never heard nobody call no Indian that before.

"He wanted to trade," Pa said. "We had us a little truce now. The Apache said mules were good, but a lot of trouble, so he was willing to trade. At first, I told him I wasn't about to trade for mules I owned."

The Apache grinned. "You do not own them," he said. I ain't sure if he said this in the Mexican lingo or with his hands. "I do."

"They belong to the Overland Mail Company, most of them." The other Apaches, about four or five, from what Pa could see, had paraded the stolen mules out for Pa and his posse to see. "The Tobiano belongs to me."

"They belong to me," the Apache said. "I stole them."

Well, as big a skinflint as Pa is, he wasn't about to trade for no mules that had been stole from him, and he told the Apache that, but the Indian didn't seem to be bothered. Must have thought it was part of the bartering.

"If you valued those mules," the Apache said, "you would not have let me take them from you. Now, they are mine. But I trade. Or we will fight, the way we fight the miners and all other pale eyes."

Pa said he cussed Ben Jakes a blue streak for letting those mules get stole.

"It's about then that I remembered it was Christmas." Pa was really in his cups by the time he got to this part of his story. I don't think he even knowed he had missed Christmas until he got back to Soldier's Farewell. Since the Apaches was mad at the miners, and not us, I think what Pa remembered in the Cedars was that, if he didn't negotiate some sort of trade, there was going to be shooting. Most likely, Pa and his friends would wind up dead.

That's when it struck me that big black mule Pa had been riding was gone.

"You traded him Boss?" I fired off at him.

Pa just nodded. "I traded him Boss, some Navy tobacco, my saddle, some bacon, coffee, all of our sugar, and Emmett Mills's hat."

"They wanted powder and shot, but we wasn't about to give them that," Cooper, the man Mr. Barney had sent along, added.

"But Boss . . . ," I started.

"And what gold coin we had on us," Pa said. "And that sorrel jenny that was too noisy, hee-hawing all the time."

I shook my head. "But they was stole. You should have fought them Indians."

"It was Red Sleeves, Smith!" Emmett Mills blurted out. "Mangas Coloradas himself!"

That shut me up. Mangas had to be the biggest Apache among the Chiricahua. For close to 30 years, he had been killing Mexicans, and, from the stories I had heard, the onliest reason he signed a treaty with the United States back in '46 was because we had just whipped the Mexicans in that war Pa had fought in, and old Mangas respected anybody who'd killed off some Mexicans. Only now, them Burchville boys had turned him into an enemy of us whites, too.

"I got Sweet Ainsley back," Pa said. "For Julian."

"And bought us some time, some peace, with Red Sleeves himself," Cooper added.

"Still . . . I mean. . . ." Not rightly sure what I meant.

Pa rose from his chair. "I'm still starved," he said, and shot a long stare at Ben Jakes. "And what we paid to get those mules back will come out of your pay, Jakes. And if it happens again, I'm delivering you to Mangas Coloradas, personally."

Same Evening, 9:15
THE UNION IS DISSOLVED!
   More later.

December 31, 1860

Back when I was a little kid of maybe five or six, I remember waking up and wondering if the lead soldiers I'd dreamt that Julian had give me was for real, or, maybe once or twice, that Ma wasn't really dead at all. But then I'd realize my hopes were forlorn—that's the word Pa used last night—and that, no, I'd just been dreaming. Sometimes, of course, I'd wake up and scoff because the dream had been so stupid I knowed it wasn't true, but oftentimes the dream seemed real and I'd have to think on it and do some considering for a little spell. So when I woke up this morning, the first thing I wondered was if everything I'd heard and witnessed last night had been a dream.

   It wasn't.

   The Union is dissolved.

   Only it ain't really all the Union, I reckon. Just South Carolina left it, although, from what I can gather, South Carolina ain't expected to be lonesome for long. "The Union is dissolved" is what some folks in Charleston wrote to say the state wasn't no part of the United States any more. Seems that a newspaper in Charleston printed those words in big letters with an exclamation mark at the end.

They brung the news on the Westbound last night, and it was all everybody talked about.

If what I heard and remember is correct, on December 20, South Carolina voted in a convention to withdraw from the United States. Voted "unanimously"—meaning that nobody there wanted to remain part of the Union. Last night's passengers, and Marco Max and Little Terry, had first heard rumors of what had happened down in Charleston when they reached Fort Chadbourne in West Texas. "Soldier boys wasn't sure what they would do, wondered what Governor Sam Houston would do down in Austin if it was true," Little Terry said. "Some didn't believe it. Marco, he wouldn't believe it, said it was just a big story."

Only that story got confirmed when they arrived at Franklin about four days later. Bunch of Texicans was firing their pistols into the ceiling at the El Paso Saloon, celebrating as if Texas had quit the Union, not South Carolina. That's what Little Terry also said he witnessed, though he attributed the fandango to "too much tangle-foot."

"I can't believe they actually did it," Marco Max kept saying over and over. "I can't believe those fools would actually secede."

"High time!" Ben Jakes exclaimed. "High time, I say, that the South got herself a divorce. Won't be long before Texas joins her independence-minded sister. Yes, sir. High time."

Well, that Celerity coach was chock-full of folks, and every last one of them had an opinion on South Carolina's actions. One gent said it was an insult, another shouted out: "As Mr. Greeley wrote . . . 'Let

them go!' " One man with a Van Dyke beard and
well-greased mustache kept trying to say something
about Senator John Crittenden's proposed amendment, how it could have prevented all this ruction. I
ain't rightly sure what that amendment was, or what
an amendment really is, or who this senator is, but
it don't really matter because the guy did manage
to get a word in that the dad-blasted Congress (he
actually used right saltier language than that) had
defeated the senator's measure.

"It's war," said a young drummer from Virginia,
and then he grinned. "Glad I'll be in Sacramento."

"It might not come to war," the only woman in
the coach said hopefully. Then closing her eyes, she
said softly: "It mustn't." Her accent sounded like she
was from Central Missouri.

"They say we can expect Louisiana and Mississippi to follow South Carolina," a man from St. Louis
said. "Alabama and Florida, too."

"And Texas!" Ben Jakes hollered. "Texas and Texicans ain't never held much truck with 'em Yankee
tyrants!"

I figured Pa would tell Ben Jakes to keep his trap
shut, but he didn't offer nothing, just let that reprobate have his say, like everyone else was having his
or her say, though the lady didn't say much at all.

"And Texas was a republic, stood by herself a long
time ago," Ben Jakes went on, as if nobody else knew
the history of the Lone Star state. "And we Texicans
ain't never been scared of no fight. We'll be right
happy to fit as many Yanks as Mr. Lincoln thinks he
can throw at us."

The man from St. Louis didn't pay Ben Jakes much
mind. "Not sure about Virginia, and other states, I
warrant, will wait to see what the Old Dominion

does. But mark my words, Missouri will leave the Union, too, and bid a fond farewell."

The lady, her eyes still closed, just shook her head.

They'd been talking a bit about the news since they knew it wasn't false in Franklin, but just a bit on account of the dust in the stagecoach, so Soldier's Farewell was the first chance they really had to speak about all this. Big news, it was. Biggest to hit the territories in a coon's age.

A gent from Ohio called the St. Louis man something, but I couldn't hear what he said because he muttered it, out of respect for the lady in earshot, but it wasn't polite. The St. Louis man didn't hear him, neither, but the Virginia drummer, sitting next to him, turned redder than one of *Señora* Dolores's hottest chiles, so it had to be mighty vulgar. Wish I could have heard what he said.

All this time, I kept shooting glances in Pa's direction after he come in from changing the team of mules, kept hoping that he might have something to opine on the matter, but he didn't opine nothing. Just sipped his coffee, asked Marco Max about the run, asked about Apaches, normal things. He sure didn't act excited like the rest of folks at the station, just went about like it was any other day.

I couldn't believe it. I mean, South Carolina was the state he was born in—at least, that's where I've always figured he entered this world. I know for sure it's where he got married, where he lived for the longest time, and where his friend Wade Hampton was serving as a senator. And now, from what I can gather, South Carolina is an independent sovereign—I heard that word last night, too— country.

Marco Max said again how he never figured

South Carolina would go through with what she'd done. Then: "I had hopes." Quietly. "I had hopes. . . ."

"Forlorn hopes," Pa told him. Then he walked outside.

January 1, 1861

A new year. Wonder what 1861 will bring to Soldier's Farewell.

January 2, 1861

More news from South Carolina came on the Westbound. The men at the secession convention in Charleston voted 169-0 to leave the Union. One of the passengers, a big, burly guy who said he was from Richmond, Virginia had a newspaper with him, and everyone—even Pa—gathered around him like he had a page from the first Bible that ever got printed. Don't know what newspaper it was, or where he bought it, because I never got close enough to see, so crowded it was. The man took the paper with him. I bet he'll be popular at every stop betwixt here and Yuma, where he said he was going.

There also was a guy from Albany, New York on the stage, and he said he figured South Carolina was not only right in leaving the Union, but other states would follow soon—far as we know, there ain't been no more states to dissolve yet—and he didn't think they would just be Southern states, too. No, he allowed he expected California might leave the Union. Even New York could find some sense in becoming independent, or so this man said.

This time Pa spoke up, after the Westbound had left. He said the man from New York was the biggest fool he'd ever seen since he come to Soldier's Farewell.

More important seems to be the question of what will happen at Fort Sumter. That's a place out in the harbor of Charleston. The commander had not surrendered it yet. Those Southrons who are spoiling for a fight down in Charleston hadn't opened fire, either, but something is bound to happen there. There was a whole article about that in the paper the burly man owned.

"Carolinians is some of the hardest fighters you'll ever tussle with," Ben Jakes said to nobody in particular. Like that was news to us. That fool Jakes must have forgot my Pa hails from South Carolina, though he left nigh 20 years ago. "Bunch of Carolinians come down to fight at the Alamo, by grab. Next news we get we'll hear that that fort ain't flying that flag of tyranny no more. And then we'll hear that Texas is free, too."

Pa spoke up again, harsher this time. "If Texas quits the Union," he said, "then you'll be out of a job."

Jakes looked up, his face white. "You'd fire me, Mr. Munro? Just because I'm for Texas?"

Pa grunted, straightened his back, and put both hands on his hips. "What do you think will happen to the Overland if Texas secedes?" He said this like he was speaking to some simpleton. Ha. I allow that he was. Ben Jakes ain't got no brains, and I ain't writing "Mr." before his name no more. I'll call him Mr., because Pa expects it, and I ain't wanting no part of one of Pa's switches, or his razor strop. No, sir.

"Well. . . ." Jakes didn't know what to say.

"The Overland has a contract with the United

States," Pa informed him. "Not the Republic of South Carolina. Not the Republic of Texas. You think they'll let us keep sending mail and people to California? If Texas goes. . . ." Pa shook his head and spit. He didn't say no more. In fact, nobody said a thing after that.

January 3, 1861

Mr. D.N. Barney come by this morning, and so did Emmett Mills and Freeman Thomas from Cooke's Spring, and a tall, skinny man named S.K. Clayton from Mimbres Stand and Mr. Dawson from Ojo de la Vaca. *Señor* Vee showed up, too. Even though he wasn't employed by the company, he's still a big man in these parts, especially after he tracked down Red Sleeves and helped get our mules back. He didn't say anything during the big meeting, however. I reckon all the important folks on the Overland between Mesilla and Stein's was here.

Luckily, as they had me making coffee and serving slumgullion and hardtack, I got to hear a lot of what they was talking about.

"La Mesilla's full of hotheads with ties to the South," Pa said.

"Anyone who reads the *Times* knows that," Emmett said.

"Tucson ain't much better," Mr. Barney said. "I wouldn't be surprised to see the southern half of New Mexico Territory declare its independence and align with the slaveholding states."

"If you read the *Times*, that's why they call this part Arizona," Emmett said. He didn't think much of the Mesilla newspaper.

"Our immediate concern is Texas," Mr. Barney

said, and he went on to say that state officials wrote up this petition, allowing how Mr. Lincoln's election was a threat to Southern rights, and they've called for a statewide election so they can send delegates to a convention this month in Austin.

Austin might be the next Charleston.

I wasn't really sure why anything that happened in Austin would do us harm at Soldier's Farewell one way or the other as we're closer to Tucson and Santa Fé than the Texas capital, but then I remembered what all Pa had said about if Texas quits the Union, then the Overland is in trouble.

"What happens to us then?" Pa looked around the table.

A couple men shook their heads. Mr. Barney drummed his fingers on the table. Finally Freeman Thomas cleared his throat. He hailed originally from New York. If you took a poll, I reckon you'd find that most of the conductors and jehus and superintendents and such come from New York. Even John Butterfield was a New Yorker. Pa once said it was on account there were so many hacks in New York, it was easy to hire men who knowed what they was doing aboard a Concord or Celerity wagon. Even Marco Max, who growed up in Vermont, learned his trade and all about stagecoaching in New York City.

"Congress wants to move the line north," Mr. Thomas said. "More of a central line, probably along the route that new Pony Express is taking."

Mr. Barney nodded his head in agreement. "Many wanted that route from the start."

"It'll be up to the Postmaster General," Mr. Thomas added.

"But he won't let the Overland's property get stole by these Rebels," Mr. Clayton said. "Will he?"

"Not likely," Pa said. "But if Texas follows South Carolina, I don't see how he can stop it."

"Be a shame," Mr. Thomas said, "to break John Butterfield's heart, to see everything he worked so hard to build fall to ruin. Southern ruin."

"John Butterfield's heart's already busted," Mr. Barney said. "Since Wells, Fargo, and Company took over the Overland."

"Well . . . what happens to us?" Mr. Dawson asked.

"The Overland can't run without stagecoaches," Pa said. "Without livestock. Can't run without men, either. I reckon they'll move us north, too."

Clayton shook his head. "Never had much desire to live in Kansas," he said.

"Let's wait and see what happens," Pa said. "It's all we can do. Just wait, and be ready."

They sipped some coffee and slurped the slumgullion, and then Emmett Mills asked Pa if he had heard from Julian. Pa just shook his head, and I recalled what Little Terry had said about the soldier boys down at Fort Chadbourne in Texas, how they wasn't sure what they would do, and I wondered if Julian and the soldiers at Fort Yuma was wondering the same, worrying.

Same day, 5:30

Pa riled me, though I didn't let on. At supper I asked him about South Carolina, and the Union being dissolved, and what this might mean to us, and he told me not to fret none, that this was a problem between the North and the South, and not New Mexico. Especially not Soldier's Farewell.

Sometimes I believe he thinks I'm just some dumb kid with no more brains than Ben Jakes.

Pa, I was inside with y'all most of the time this morn whilst y'all was talking about these things! I heard practically everything said!

That's what I wanted to yell at him, but I'm good at holding my tongue.

What about Julian? How's these events going to affect him? He's in the U.S. Dragoons! And he's our family.

I didn't say none of that, neither.

Too mad to sleep right now. Too mad to write any more, also.

I ain't stupid, Pa!

January 4, 1861

Got a letter from Julian. Well, it wasn't much of a letter. Only one page, with him saying he was glad to hear Pa hadn't gotten kilt by Apaches, and he thanked us for saving Sweet Ainsley, apologized for not writing us sooner, and, finally, he closed with a sentence about everything happening back East.

I guess you have heard about South Carolina.

That was it. Figured he'd have more to say on all the goings on. Hoped he would, as maybe that would spark some comment from Pa. No luck, though. Well, I suspect Julian's right busy. Probably tired.

As for Pa, well, he ain't been talking much about anything lately.

January 5, 1861

The Velásquez family come over, and *Señora* Dolores brung us some *menudo*. It's a soup. I ain't one to complain, and I managed to get my bowl full down, but I'm certain sure I don't want to know what she puts in that soup, because it's about the only thing I've ever tasted that makes me long for Pa's slumgullion.

Tori didn't act up none during the short visit. Alyvia asked about Julian, and Pa read his letter, not that it was much of a letter. Alyvia just nodded silently as Pa read. I wonder where *Señor* Vee and his family stands in this whole mess, if they are for the Union or for Southern rights.

Same day, quarter past 8, evening

Reread what I wrote about *Señor* Vee this morning, and that has me thinking, and writing, again as it brings to mind stories Pa and Julian every now and then would tell me about the Revolution, where we won our independence from King George and England. Some of it was wrote about in one of those books by Mr. Simms, but we ain't got but one of Simms's books no more and it ain't about the war against the British. During that fracas, they say there was a lot of wild happenings in Camden, South Carolina, and that area, that folks would question neighbors if they was for the Patriots or on the King's side, and if you answered wrong, you might get tarred and feathered, whipped, burned out, or even killed.

I wonder if it'll ever come to that with this confrontation between North and South.

January 6, 1861

From listening to the grown-ups talk about things, it seems that South Carolina and any other states that decide to dissolve won't be sovereign countries. A lot of folks think when Mr. Lincoln replaces James Buchanan (Andrew Jackson ain't President, after all), he'll fight to preserve the Union. So the South will band together as a Confederacy. I heard that word mentioned on the Westbound.

Still no word on anything happening at Fort Sumter. South Carolina wants the Federal troops to get out, but President Buchanan says he ain't doing no such thing.

January 9, 1861

Don't reckon Texas will be the next state to secede, after all. Word from the Westbound is that there's a big meeting in Mississippi. Florida, Alabama, Georgia, and Louisiana have all called for conventions, too.

January 10, 1861

Rained this morning. Cold and windy.

January 11, 1861

Eastbound stage was about as crowded as I can remember ever seeing it, and that's saying something because there appears to be a lot of folks going East now, or have been since news about South Carolina reached the territories and California. Only this time, there was a soldier boy, a baldheaded captain in the Navy who had left San Francisco and had resigned his commission. He got out to stretch his legs whilst we was changing the team of mules—Pa didn't like that none, but let it go, this time—and struck up a conversation with Ben Jakes, who was shirking his duties as usual, and said he could not protect the interests of the Union no more when his family and friends and home state were being threatened.

He's from South Carolina, and he talked a lot until a Yankee inside the stage yelled that he'd best shut up.

Thought there might be a fight, but the sailor tightened his lips and said nothing more, and Pa told the former captain that he'd best climb back inside the coach. Right about then there come up a little shower.

Pa just looked real sad at that sailor as he got back inside. Jakes hollered at him to kill a score of Yankees at Fort Sumter for him. The Navy captain said he prayed it wouldn't never come to that.

Then the stagecoach took off, and we turned in. Rain stopped. Can't sleep.

January 12, 1861

Apaches killed two men traveling to the Pinos Altos mines from Mowry City. *Señor* Vee discovered their bodies, and lit a shuck back here to tell us the news. Pa rode out with Ben Jakes and *Señor* Vee to bury those guys. They got back as quick as they could, then *Señor* Vee rode off at a high lope to get back to his family. Can't blame him none for that.

Nobody's talking about South Carolina and the South and Mr. Lincoln any more. Got enough troubles. Pa ordered an extra guard each night to protect our mules. Don't want Sweet Ainsley stole again.

January 13, 1861

No sign of any Apaches. Mules and livestock all safe here.

January 16, 1861

Mississippi has joined South Carolina. Word come quicker this time. But not many people talked about it. Those deaths of those two men must have reminded everyone that the Apaches are a bigger concern in New Mexico Territory, or Arizona Territory if you want to call it that, than what's going on in South Carolina and Mississippi.

Still no sign of Apaches. Wonder if those two guys who got killed were done in by Red Sleeves, old Mangas Coloradas himself. If so, he's keeping his peace with the Overland.

Glad I ain't a miner.

January 17, 1861

Ben Jakes says he heard Apaches while he was on guard duty last night, but he run them off. Nobody believes him.

January 18, 1861

Latest Apache scare seems to be fading away. Or was, at least, for me, until the Eastbound come in. Pa give the jehu a leather bundle, asked him if he'd see it got delivered to a Mrs. Luz Blanco in La Mesilla.

I asked him what it was and who was Luz Blanco, and he frowned, then said it was a letter and some personal belongings that he and *Señor* Vee had discovered on one of the fellows the Apaches had killed. Stuff the Indians hadn't stole off him.

"What about the other dead man?" I asked.

Pa shook his head. "Nothing," he said.

That got me to fretting. I mean, Pa and *Señor* Vee didn't find nothing that could tell them who this dead man was. Maybe Mrs. Blanco knows who her husband was traveling to the mines with, but what if she don't? Then this man, he's going to be buried for all eternity with not even a name over his grave. His wife, or his ma and pa might not ever know what become of him. That's sad.

Sometimes Soldier's Farewell seems to be the loneliest spot in the whole world.

January 19, 1861

Snowed. Just another dusting. Wind's blowing like a hurricane, and it's bitter, bitter cold. Don't think we have to worry about Apaches, not in this weather. Ain't fit to be outside.

January 20, 1861

More news from the South from the Westbound. Florida and Alabama are gone, Georgia's expected to secede—might already have done so by the time I write this—and there's a meeting in Louisiana later this month. Rumors are that the Southern states will meet in Montgomery, Alabama, and form a new nation. Plus Governor Sam Houston has called for a big meeting of the legislature tomorrow in Austin, Texas.

Mr. Lincoln, it is said, might not even live long enough to become President. Since he got elected, maybe even before then, folks have been saying how they'll kill him.

One man from Baton Rouge on the stagecoach tonight said only Lincoln's death could prevent a war. He said it would be a just death, too.

"Would that be enough to reunite North and South?" a schoolteacher bound for San Felipe asked.

"It's too late for reconciliation, sir," the Baton Rouge fire-eater fired back. "Much too late."

Also, learned that, on the 9th of this month, shots were fired on this ship called the *Star of the West* that President Buchanan had sent to help the garrison at Fort Sumter. The ship wasn't damaged none, but now folks are saying there will surely be a war.

Thinking a lot about Julian.

So's Pa. Only he won't say it. He don't say much these days. But today, long before the Westbound stage come through, I watched him, whittling, leaning against the tall stone wall, staring at that old ragged flag that was popping like musketry in the wind. Cold as it was, windy as tarnation he didn't notice none of that. He just looked at that flag.

'Course, he might have been thinking about the first two states he called home, South Carolina and Mississippi, and how they ain't part of the United States any more, but I reckon I know he was thinking about Brother Jules. About the war folks say can't be stopped now.

Was I to ask him about it, Pa'd just tell me that no war between North and South would ever come to the territory, but he'd be lying.

It's Sunday, so Pa made me recite some Scripture today. He just stared at me as I spoke the words of Jesus from The Gospel According to St. Matthew.

"'And ye shall hear of wars and rumors of wars; see that ye be not troubled. . . .'"

Before I could finish, Pa joined in. He'd never done that before. Sometimes I didn't think he knowed one verse from the Bible, but this time he started talking, just a whisper, but he was speaking with me, then, when I quit after just a few words, he finished the whole verse by himself.

"'For all these things must come to pass, but the end is not yet.'"

January 21, 1861

Quiet day of chores. While Pa and the boys worked on the stables, repairing some fence, I had to head to the spring and fix the dam, pile on some more stones.

Good day, if cold. Nobody talking about the North, nobody talking about the South, nobody talking about Apaches.

Nobody talking, but I warrant all them things are heavy on most grown-ups' minds. Heavy on my mind, too.

January 22, 1861

Tuesday Eastbound came in an hour behind schedule, and Pa was hopping mad. Wind blowing like a gale, kicking up dust in the darkness. Couldn't see hardly a thing, and cold as it kept getting, that wind would suck the life out of you.

Mules begun balking—that no-account gray jenny even tried to sit on her hindquarters, but she wasn't the only one acting stubborn, stubborner than Pa, meaning both the teams we was unhitching and the fresh ones Bartolomé and Ben Jakes was bringing out of the stables. Couldn't blame them none. Nobody wanted to be out in this weather.

"Come on! Quit lollygagging!" Pa barked. "We can't afford to lose more time!"

Some folks say a jackman must be as patient as an oyster and that you almost got to be if you want to raise mules, and Pa is oftener tolerant when he's working with his animals. By jingo, I've knowed him to let a stallion run along with a jenny for upwards of six years before that jenny ever got in the family way and delivered us another mule. But ain't no station boss forgiving when working on the Overland, and when one of the passengers jumped down from the top off the Celerity wagon, Pa just about bust his gut.

Soon as the gent landed with a grunt, Pa had whirled around from the mules Bartolomé and Ben Jakes was bringing to the wagon tongue. When the newcomer called up for one of the other passengers unfortunate enough to have to ride up top if he'd toss down his carpetbag, Pa had had enough.

"What in blazes are you doing?" Pa yelled to the fellow in the shadows. "This ain't no leg-stretching stop. Get back on board, Mr., or you'll be walking to wherever you're going!"

He turned back, and shouted at me to give a hand, so I run from helping Mr. Fletcher, and conductor Donnie O'Donnell put the tired team in the stables, and started harnessing the fresh team to the coach.

My lips was cracked from the wind and cold, my fingers felt frozed, and I could barely breathe from the dust and weather.

When we got the team all hitched, Ben Jakes and me, working the right side of the coach, stepped back. Above the wind, I heard Pa yelling at the man that had jumped down off the coach to get back up, *muy pronto,* and then Big Terry, who was driving the Eastbound, just let out a belly laugh before firing out a stream of cusses as he popped that whip of his. The Celerity took off, kicking up more dust that I had to swallow, and disappeared in the blackness of the night.

The man in the shadows just stood there, holding a bag in one hand and what looked to be a rifle in the other.

"Mr., this better be your stop, you blamed idiot," Pa told the passenger who'd just got left behind, "because the only way you can get aboard another Eastbound is if there's room. And there ain't been a whole lot of room on any Eastbound coach the past two weeks."

With a nonchalant attitude, the man just flipped his carpetbag toward our little home. He took a couple of steps so that the light from the lantern on the post hit him.

"Maybe now," he said, "you can see a little better."

He wasn't dressed nothing like when I had last

seen him. Even in the dark, I allow I would have recognized him had he been wearing that cloth shako
of the dragoons. Atop Julian's head was a black slouch
hat, dusty, battered and ripped in a couple of places
along the front with a patch of crossed sabers—which
had become regulation back in 1850—sewn into the
crown. None of which I really seen till later. Instead
of the blue woolen jacket with orange trim and brass
epaulettes, he wore what we called back in Missouri
a hunter's shirt, long, heavy gray flannel with the
scales sewn on the shoulders to reveal his rank. His
blue britches of kersey wool were stuffed in black
boots, and he wore brass spurs and a black belt over
his waist with a Colt revolver in the holster. No saber on him, although, later, I spotted it sheathed in
its scabbard and tied to the bag he had tossed toward the door, but he held a 1847 musketoon in his
left hand.

Nobody moved, not at first, just stood staring at
the young man standing in the light.

Pa whispered my brother's name, and took a tenta-
tive step forward, then stopped, just staring while the
wind blew so hard it bent one side of Julian's black
hat up against the crown, and kept at it till Julian had
to press the hat down on his head with his free hand
to keep it from blowing all the way to old Mexico.

"Julian," Pa said again, only he still hadn't got his
legs to working.

He looked different, my brother did, and it wasn't
just all the makeshift uniform either. He wasn't a
cadet fresh off the Hudson no more. Older, I reckon.
Wiser. Maybe even harder. Chasing Paiutes will do
that to any fellow. He had started growing this mustache before he took off to Fort Tejon, but back then

it had looked mostly like dirty peach fuzz. Emmett Mills had even joked that Jules wouldn't need no razor to shave that thing off, that warm water would do the job. Now the mustache wasn't fuzz. I ain't writing that it was as big and brushy as Mr. Fletcher's, although Julian's wasn't yet so stained by tobacco juice and my brother hadn't grown a beard to go with it and Julian's hair was brown, not the color of sandstone like Mr. Fletcher's, but Julian's dark mustache wasn't something you'd overlook or joke about, neither.

It struck me then, in the dark, staring at my big brother.

Julian Munro had growed into a man.

I'm sitting here, scratching this while the memories are still in my head, waiting for Pa and Julian to finish talking about things so my brother, Lieutenant Munro, can come to bed. I'm supposed to be asleep, but it's too exciting to sleep now with my brother back home.

Home.

Never figured I'd call Soldier's Farewell home, but it is. Especially now that our family is back together again.

With the sight of Julian registering at last, I shouted out something, a cheer, maybe, I really don't know, but Pa came forward first, moving at last, holding out his right hand, as if he were going to shake Julian's hand, then rushing the final few rods, extending his left hand, and grasping my brother in a bear hug, laughing, twisting his first-born son around in a circle.

Calling Julian a dirty name, Pa finally released his

grip and dropped Julian back to his feet and yelled: "Don't you know how to write? Why didn't you let us know you was coming?"

"Thought I'd surprise y'all."

"Uhn-huh." Pa stood there, sizing Julian up. "I knew a man back in Mississippi, decided he'd surprise his father and mother. Went home, walked in the door, and got his arm blowed off at the elbow by his daddy's shotgun. Yes, sir, that turned out to be quite a surprise."

"I'm glad you don't greet passengers with a shotgun."

"No. No, I reckon we're a tad less nervous, and a whole lot friendlier here."

"Uhn-huh." Julian grinned. "I've seen and heard how friendly you are here." He puffed out his chest, put his hands on his hips, and gave a right fair imitation of Pa's boisterous voice: "Mr., this better be your stop, you blamed idiot. . . . This ain't no leg-stretching stop, what in Sam Hill are you doing? . . . Quit lollygagging! We can't afford to lose any more time!"

Mr. Fletcher let out a chuckle over that, adding: "That's about the size of it." Which got Ben Jakes, Bartolomé, and Julian laughing like coyotes, and I soon joined in. After the longest while, Pa started cackling, too. Then we all stopped, but only for a second before Pa roared out again, slapping his thighs, and we joined him a-laughing and a-laughing till at last Pa stopped and said: "Let's get out of the wind."

Everyone come inside, shaking my brother's hand, telling him it was good to see him, how fine he looked, all that kind of stuff, while I hauled in my brother's grip—that's when I noticed the saber in its silver scabbard tied to the carpetbag—and Pa fetched a jug. I set Julian's bag in the corner and took the musketoon from him without comment, which I leaned against the wall beside his flowery carpetbag and shiny saber. As my brother unbuckled his gun belt, Pa poured Julian a glass, but he wasn't about to dirty up dishes for the rest of us, so the jug got passed around. He even let Ben Jakes have a snort, but snatched it from my hands when Ben Jakes passed it to me.

"Ah, Pa . . . ," I said, but not too loud on account I didn't want to spoil his mood.

"How long you here?" Mr. Fletcher asked. "You on leave?"

"New orders." Julian done some smacking and wiped his lips. "That'll age you." He studied the glass.

"Fort Tejon whiskey's better?" Pa inquired, as if he had just been insulted.

"Well," Julian said, "I ain't blind."

Eyes sparkling, Mr. Fletcher added: "Yet."

Which started them all guffawing again.

Pa asked Jules if he was hungry, and we warmed up some stew and coffee and ate us a late meal, with Mr. Fletcher, Ben Jakes, and Bartolomé calling it a night after they'd all had themselves a snort, telling Julian it was good to see him again, and then they filed out into the dark and went to their own bunks, leaving us Munros alone.

Nobody spoke while Jules filled his belly—we just stared at him, noticing how he looked, how he had changed, maybe just marveling at the sight of him, speechless the whole time—although I was right eager to pepper him with questions, and finally he slid the empty bowl away from him and said: "You're awful quiet, Smith. Cat got your tongue?"

"You going to see Alyvia?" Dumb. Just plain

ignorant, but that's the only thing I could think of to ask right then and there, even though I was loaded up with questions, good questions, and stories I wanted to hear him tell.

"Now?" he asked, all surprised, and Pa tried not to laugh but couldn't hold it in his mouth. "It's a bit late to go. . . ."

Pa finished for him. "Courting?" He laughed at the following silence, which I broke.

"Well . . . what are you doing here?" I asked Julian. Then I got a little frightened. "You didn't run off, did you?"

Raking his rough hands through my hair, Julian shook his head and shot Pa a wink. "You're afraid I'm going to steal your bunk and make you sleep on the floor? Is that it?"

"No." I started to tell him that the floor would probably be more comfortable than my bed, but decided against that.

"You look different," I said.

"I feel different," he said, only he said it different, too, but I don't think Pa, or even Julian, noticed the change in his voice.

"You must be tired," Pa said.

"A Celerity wagon isn't the most comfortable conveyance," Julian agreed.

"Uhn-huh. You didn't answer Smith's question," Pa said. "Did you run off?" I spotted a glitter in Pa's eye.

"It's like I told Fletcher," Julian replied. "New orders."

"Can you tell me about fighting Paiutes?" I asked. I'd interrupted them, and Pa didn't like it none.

"Time for bed," he told me. "Don't worry. Julian can feed your appetite for war stories. . . ." He turned to my brother. "For how long?"

"I have plenty of time to tell some windies," he said. "I have two months' leave before reporting for assignment. Thought I'd stay here."

"You can ride Sweet Ainsley!" I suggested.

"I'd love to ride her."

Pa asked: "Where will you be going from here?"

Julian didn't answer for a while. He drummed his fingers, staring at them, and it looked to me like he started to reach for the jug Bartolomé had set on the table, but slowly withdrew that hand, and looked up at Pa.

"East," was all he said.

About then's when Pa sent me to bed, which ain't fair, however Pa wasn't in any mood for delays so I didn't tarry. It ain't like I could sleep, knowing Julian was back home, that he and Pa were probably drinking more from that jug of mescal and talking about important matters. Writing these words, I can still hear him and Julian talking, although I can't make out none of their words.

I got a good notion what the conversation's about. The war. The shooting war that's coming about on account of the South pulling out of the Union. Julian's heading East, and that means he won't be fighting Paiutes, or Apaches, or some other red Indian. He won't be fighting the Mexicans, like Pa done in the big war before I was born. I recall one of those conversations I'd overheard here at the station after we got word about South Carolina dissolving the Union, although I can't remember who said it or when, but it strikes me that it must have been just a couple of days ago and from that schoolteacher who had taken a job in San Felipe, California.

"My fear is that you are correct, and that there will be war, unavoidable war, and this war will be like none we have ever seen on this continent. It will be a war of fathers fighting sons, brothers fighting brothers. I tremble at the thought."

I'm trembling now.

Same night, later, not sure of the time

Julian come in, the sharp stink of mescal on his breath. I wonder if there's any of that liquor left in the jug. He was pulling off his boots when I rolled over.

"Didn't mean to wake you, Smith," he whispered.

"I wasn't sleeping."

"Well, that's good." He tossed his boots, spurs still on, into the corner. "Pa says I can have your bed. You can sleep on the floor." He slapped my thigh. "Might as well move now. I'm tuckered out."

"You're in your cups."

"A tad. If you want to sleep in the bed. . . ."

"No." I sat up. "It's all right." I didn't tell him about the floor being more comfortable. He tossed his hat toward his boots, and started unbuttoning his hunter's shirt.

"You and Pa talked quite a bit."

"Too much," Julian said. "I'm worn out."

"You're going East?"

He left his hand on the heavy flannel, just looking out at nothing. "Yeah," he said after the longest while, and pulled off the garment.

"They say there will be a war," I said. "Between the North and the South."

"I'd say they're right." He still wasn't looking at me. Now he started on his pants.

"Reckon that troubles Pa," I said.

He laughed, but it wasn't nothing like the laughs from earlier this night. In fact, it sounded more bitter than anything else. "I told Pa that I got just as much chance of getting killed by a Paiute arrow as I do from a white man back . . . wherever."

"Maybe not," I said hopefully. "There was this fellow from Baton Rouge on the stage, and he was saying that, if there was a war, it wouldn't be much of a war, that it would only last a week or two, a month at the most. You might still be here by the time all the shooting is stopped."

He didn't say a thing, just pulled off them soldier pants of his.

"You don't believe that?" I asked. I had to repeat the question before he answered me.

Now he turned, holding folded pants and shirt in his hands, sitting on the bunk in his winter drawers and socks. He just looked at me, looked at me the longest while, and I wasn't sure he had an answer. In fact, for a little bit I thought he might start to crying, but it was fairly dark in the room, and I was pretty tired myself.

"I . . . I don't know what to believe, Smith," he said. "Not any more."

Well, I couldn't come up with words to all that. Didn't even try.

"You keep the bed tonight," Julian told me. "Chasing Indians with Captain Carleton, I'm used to sleeping on hard ground."

He crossed the room, weaving some, didn't even bother taking a blanket with him, and laid down in the corner, using his folded clothes for a pillow, not even covering himself.

"This one fellow," I said, still sitting, "he said it would be a war like nothing we'd ever seen in America. He said it would be a war of brothers fighting brothers."

He rolled over, dark eyes locked on me.

"That scares you?" he asked.

I shrugged.

"I wouldn't fight you, Smith," he said.

"Good," I said, trying to make him laugh again. I mean, this was supposed to be a happy reunion, and here we were talking about war, and not all the glory of fighting in the Army and stuff, but bad thoughts. Seems that everyone traveling along the Overland had nothing but bad thoughts, or mean thoughts about other Americans. "Because I'd hate to have to whup you, Jules."

He laughed. "I won't give you the chance, baby Brother. Now go to sleep."

"Pa says he don't think the war will ever come to New Mexico Territory," I said. I didn't tell him about how, in some ways, the war had already come this way, with people fighting amongst each other, didn't tell him that there was a chance the Overland would even move the route out of New Mexico and up into Kansas or some place like that.

"Go to sleep," he said again, rolling over. Pretty soon, all I heard was the snores of Julian. Then it seemed like I heard footsteps, as if Pa had been listening to us talking, spying on us, and now he was walking away. Maybe that was my imagination.

Now I can hear the snores of both my father and my brother. I'm sitting here on my bed, writing in this bunk, although it's blasted hard to see right now.

Can't sleep.

January 30, 1861

By jacks, more than a week has passed since I last wrote in this diary. Guess that shows how busy things have been around here. Stagecoaches, both them heading east and those going west, have all been full of passengers and lots of mail. It brings to mind this story from a San Antonio newspaper—the *Herald* was its name, I think—that a passenger showed us when we first got here and the Overland started running in '58.

To make excellent jam; squeeze six or eight women, now-a-days, into a common stagecoach.

I thought about that, also, on account of the jam *Señora* Dolores brung. It ain't all been work, you see. On Monday, the 28th, Pa throwed a *baile* for Julian, and the whole Velásquez gang come. Emmett Mills, he was there, too, and *Señora* Dolores brought enough food to fill a whole brigade's bellies. The jam she made out of prickly pear, and I don't reckon I've ever had anything so tasty, at least, not since leaving Missouri. Julian kept teasing me after I'd spread some jam on one of her *tortillas* and was eating it all up, saying that I'd better watch for the cactus spines as I might get one stuck in my tongue.

Things couldn't get finer.

Things couldn't get any finer than that party, or the past week.

Julian has been working with me some on my grammar—how I talk, how I write, teaching me things like subject and verb agreement, avoiding the usage of double negatives like I started to write just above. It's hard, but when he opened his carpetbag the day after he arrived, he pulled out a *McGuffey's*

New Fourth Ecletic Reader, even though I never saw a *Third Reader* but had read the first two of those books before we left Missouri, and we've been practicing and reading it each night. Julian's a pretty good teacher, and patient.

He's also one mighty fine dancer. Everybody at the *baile* marveled about how he could dance. He and Alyvia danced just about every dance there was with *Señor* Vee sawing his fiddle and Emmett Mills banging out a tune on his jaw's harp while Ben Jakes proved he ain't totally worthless as he brought out his spoons and kept time. Sounded good, too.

We played, sang, and danced to just about everything, from minstrel tunes like "Darling Nelly Gray" and "The Flag of Our Union" to songs I could belt out real loud like "Do They Miss Me at Home?", "Pop Goes the Weasel", and "Buffalo Gals". We danced to "Woodman, Spare That Tree", which Pa said is his favorite (I never knew that, never even heard him sing till that day), and "From Greenland's Icy Mountains", "Old Folks at Home"—a lot of Stephen Foster songs, I'd say—and some California songs Julian had learned at Fort Tejon, though I couldn't tell you what they were called, and at least two were in Spanish. They even played some songs by this fellow named Chopin. Tried to, anyhow.

The best part happened when Julian brought out a protesting *Señora* Dolores to cut the rug one time to Virginia reel. *Señor* Vee laughed and laughed as his wife pleaded, in Spanish and English, with Julian not to make her dance, but finally, with her girls urging her, she bowed graciously, and her husband sawed that fiddle.

Laughing herself after a while, the *señora* showed us all that she knew how to dance mighty fine, too, and when the reel ended, she was sweating. Sweating in January! Well, it has warmed up a mite, but not that much.

"Is that what they taught you at Fort Tejon?" Emmett Mills asked my brother, who had yet to sit out one dance.

"He didn't learn to dance from the Paiutes, I warrant," Mr. Fletcher said.

"Polkas, waltzes, quadrilles, mazurkas," Julian said. "An officer and a gentleman should know them all, although I had to teach my superiors the Carolina promenade."

Twice, I danced with Tori, and she wasn't . . . wasn't a nuisance.

Everyone had worked up an appetite by the time we'd finished dancing, and while we will usually eat some of *Señora* Dolores's leftovers after she brings us some grub, a body would have been pressed mighty hard to find even a crumb after we had eaten second and third helpings. Dancing makes you hungry.

Just about the most fun we've had at Soldier's Farewell in a coon's age.

Westbound's due tonight. Back to work.

January 31, 1861

Julian has gone off to see Alyvia, but told me to practice my writing in my diary, and that he wanted to see what I wrote when he got home. I thought about writing nothing. That would teach him a lesson. However, I guess I should practice, show my brother that he's a good teacher, and write about how great things have been now that he has come home.

Maybe he will feel guilty and I'll get my bed back.

February 2, 1861

I didn't write last night after the Eastbound left. Mainly because I was troubled. Still feel troubled. As pleasant as things have been since my brother returned home, last night turned downright savage. Now, I ain't . . . I'm not one to feel sorry for Ben Jakes, but. . . .

It happened like this.

The Eastbound pulled in right on time, and Julian helped out, bringing the fresh team of mules from the stables, and this fellow, riding atop the coach on account it was crowded with people, he called out: "Julian Munro, by the saints, is that you?"

Julian looked up, but on account of the dark, couldn't make out the fellow's face.

"Bucky Sullivan!" He stood up, wobbling atop the stage, and I thought he might step down, which would really rile Pa, but he didn't. He wore a shako and what looked like a striking military jacket, so I knew he was in the Army before he called out his rank. Seems that he had been serving in the dragoons as an officer at Fort Yuma, and I guess he and Julian had fought Paiutes together.

"Captain. . . ." Julian stopped, unsure, and stepped away from the mules.

"It's no longer, Captain, Mr. Munro," the passenger said, "but it will be Colonel Sullivan when I return home to Savannah." He sat down, and the stagecoach started with a jolt, heading into the night as Sullivan yelled out: "Georgia will never yield to tyrants! Huh-rah! Huh-rah for Southern liberty!"

Well, Julian just stood there, brushing off the dust, watching the darkness swallow the Celerity wagon, and Ben Jakes walked up to him.

"Friend of yourn?" Ben Jakes asked. There wasn't any pleasantness in his voice, so I knew right away that Ben Jakes had bitten off a mouthful of trouble.

"I know him."

"You might have to kill him," Ben Jakes said. "Afore long. You think about that, Munro, when you're fightin' for the Yankees. You might kill him, your pard, a good Georgia patriot, or he might kill you!"

Whirling, cursing, Julian swung and rocked Ben Jakes with a hammer-like fist under the chin. It's a miracle he didn't break that no-account's jaw. One punch was all Julian needed. The thing is—Julian didn't stop with that one punch.

Ben Jakes staggered back, somehow kept his feet, but he never lifted his arms—guess he had been stunned—and Julian pounced on him, hit him again and again and again, in the head, chest, stomach, knocking him backward until Ben Jakes fell against the stone building.

"I . . . quit. . . ." That's all Ben Jakes managed to say, but Julian didn't listen. I don't think he even heard. Acted like a hydrophoby wolf, just crazy. Crazy and mean. He landed a right that smashed Jakes's nose into a bloody pulp, forcing Jakes's head hard against the stone wall, so hard I thought my brother had knocked the fool's skull apart.

Wheezing, Julian stepped back, and I thought he'd let it go, but he didn't. When Ben Jakes started to sink to the ground, Julian grabbed him by his shirt front, lifted him up, and leaned him against the wall, then hit him. Again. And again. Ben Jakes couldn't say anything by then. In the light, I saw his face, or what had been his face. His eyes had already swollen shut, his lips and nose just mangled flesh, but Julian kept pounding him.

"No mas" Bartolomé added. *"No mas, por favor."*

Julian's reply came with a left that crushed Jakes's ear and felled him to the ground. The blowhard didn't move, but Julian did.

He kicked him, kicked him hard in the chest, and the snapping of ribs almost made me lose my supper.

"Julian!" I yelled. Mr. Fletcher and Bartolomé wouldn't move. Later, I heard Mr. Fletcher explain to Pa that it wasn't his fight, and that he had been raised better and knew better than to stick his nose in something that wasn't his affair.

It was my affair, though. If I didn't stop Julian, he might beat Ben Jakes to death, and I sure didn't want to see my brother hang for murder.

"Stop it!" I leaped behind him, tried to grab his arms, but Julian tossed me off, easy, like I was a feather, and I landed in the dirt with a thud.

"Stop, Jules! You'll kill him!" I clambered back to my feet, deciding to tackle Julian, wrapping my arms around his legs before he could kick the unconscious man again. He went down, crashing violently for I had surprised him, but quickly pulled out of my grip, and started up, moving back for Ben Jakes.

I rolled over, scrambling to get up, then saw Julian tumbling back toward the wall, away from Ben Jakes, and it took a while before I realized that Ben Jakes hadn't knocked my brother. Not hardly, Ben Jakes wasn't moving. I thought he might not even be breathing.

Pa done it.

Julian put out his arms to stop himself from smashing into those heavy stones, pushed himself away, and turned back.

"Leave it go, Son! He's finished!"

Pa, who had been in the stables, stood there,

a mountain, and maybe Julian finally heard. He slowed, stopped, just stood, trying to catch his breath, letting everything that had just happened register. After the longest while, he brought his skinned knuckles to his mouth.

"Help your brother up," Pa told Julian.

"I don't need no help!" I fired back, forgetting all about those grammar lessons Julian had been teaching me, and climbed to my feet.

"You hurt?" Pa asked.

"I'm all right, but. . . ." I glanced at Ben Jakes, and sighed with relief when I detected his stomach rising and falling.

"Get him inside," Pa ordered Bartolomé and Mr. Fletcher. "What started all this?"

He was looking at Julian when he asked that, but Julian didn't attempt an answer, so I cleared my throat and told Pa what all had happened. It didn't seem much excuse for a fight, at least not something as savagesome as I had just witnessed, but when I had finished my account, Pa's head bobbed ever so slightly.

"I'm going for a ride," Julian announced. He headed toward the stables.

"It's after midnight!" I called out. "There's Apaches and. . . ."

"Let him go," Pa told me quietly, staring after Julian. "Let him ride it out. He'll be all right."

Then we went to check on Ben Jakes.

February 3, 1861

Julian didn't come back till this evening—and I ain't ashamed to write that I have been scared, fearing he might have run into Red Sleeves or some other contrary Apache—but he rode up right before the Westbound arrived. Good thing, because we needed him to lend a hand as Ben Jakes is off his feet with five or six busted ribs, broken nose, split lips. He swallowed two, three teeth Julian knocked out, too.

Pa expects him to be laid up for a couple of weeks. Knowing Ben Jakes the way I do, I figure he'll stay in his bunk three or four weeks, and it'll be me waiting on him, bringing him his meals, even having to empty his chamber pot. Thought of tending him like that just makes my gut spin.

Nobody said a thing about the ruction, at least not when I was around, but I'm certain sure Pa and Julian had a discussion in the stables after the Westbound went on its way. Don't know what they said, though, and I'm not in the mood to ask Julian about it and know better than to question Pa.

February 4, 1861

Julian rode off on Sweet Ainsley to see Alyvia and the Velásquez family this morning, and when he got back early this evening, he helped me through the *Reader* and we practiced writing and such.

Things getting back to normal.

February 5, 1861

Don't miss Ben Jakes at all around here, not with Julian helping. The Eastbound come, 10 minutes early, and got off without a hitch. Bartolomé told Julian that if he wanted to resign his commission, he was right certain Wells, Fargo, & Company would have a place for him on the Overland.

I laughed, but Julian acted like he hadn't heard, and walked off to the stables, and trotted off on Sweet Ainsley without another word. About three, four hours later, he rode back, climbing into the bed— I'm still sleeping on the floor now—and whispered something to himself. Maybe he was praying.

Something's bothering him, and I know what it is, least ways think I do. He's worrying about what he done to Ben Jakes, ashamed that I had seen that side of him. If he had stopped, if he had just knocked some sense into Ben Jakes, that would have been one thing, but the way he tore into Ben Jakes, that wasn't an officer and a gentleman and West Point graduate. He acted more like some monster. But things are better now. I'm glad.

February 6, 1861

We hear of trouble among the Indians around Apache Pass, and even more bad news come on tonight's Westbound. Texas has joined South Carolina, Mississippi, and all the other states that have left the Union. More later.

February 7, 1861

On February 1, the folks down in Austin voted to join the Confedcracy. That's the word we got last night. That means seven states have already dissolved the Union: South Carolina, Mississippi, Florida, Alabama, Georgia, Louisiana, and Texas. The passengers on the stage last night all agreed that Arkansas, Tennessee, and North Carolina would also leave, but Virginia sparked debate. So did Kentucky, and Missouri, but most of the talk concerned Virginia, although I had more interest in Missouri, it being the place of my birth and where I'd grown up before leaving for the territory.

Today, however, everyone wanted to talk about Texas. That's why Pa saddled up the big old Percheron and rode off to Barney's Station with Freeman Thomas from Cooke's Spring, and Bill Dawson from Ojo de la Vaca. Mr. Barney had called a big meeting to talk about what Texas's secession will mean for the Overland, similar, I guess, to the meeting Pa held here a while back.

Julian, though, he didn't have much to say on the matter, even when Mr. Fletcher pried him on it. Instead, he just set me down at the table so we could practice reading and writing.

Same day, 9:30 p.m.

Pa got back, and Julian asked how the meeting went, and Pa just shrugged. "We wait," he answered, fetching a new jug.

"Seems like the whole country's doing that," Julian offered.

"Seems like," Pa agreed. He held up the clay jug. "Thirsty?"

Julian shook his head, and motioned me to follow him. So we retired to our room, me on the floor, Julian in my bed, and Pa at the table, alone.

February 9, 1861

I've just got to write about the newcomer, a raw-boned tall *hombre* who got off the Eastbound last night. He's come to help us, and we sure need an extra hand what with Ben Jakes all stove up from that pounding Julian given him.

"Soldier's Farewell!" Marco Max called out to his passengers as the stagecoach pulled in about 15 minutes late. "We'll be changing teams, so hold your horses. You can stretch your legs and visit the privy at Cooke's down the pike if we make up some lost time!"

Yet almost before he had finished his speech and set the brake, this gent hops down from inside. "Reckon I'll stay here, driver."

Hearing those words, I pulled away from the rigging I had been working on, helping Bartolomé unhitch the team, and warned the stranger, who I couldn't see too well in midnight black. "You might not be able to catch another stage, Mr., for a spell. Coaches have been jammed full of folks of late."

"Reason I'm gettin' off," he said, brushing dust off his clothes with a wide-brimmed sombrero. "I'm a man who needs air to breathe."

"This ain't a hotel!" Pa, bringing out the harnessed fresh team with Julian and Mr. Fletcher, barked out those words, and the tall stranger straightened and stared into the darkness toward the shadow that was Pa.

"I expect to earn my keep." The man settled the hat back on his head, then just jumped right in and helped me with the mules. Well, we got the teams changed, put the tuckered-out span in the stables, and long before we had finished our chores, Marco

Max had pulled out, so the stranger was stranded here, unless he wanted to take the "ankle express" to wherever he was bound, and with Apaches acting ornery, that wasn't exactly a healthy choice.

Bartolomé went to his bunk, and I walked alongside the stranger back to our house, where I knew Pa would be waiting. Had to walk mighty fast to keep up with the long-legged fellow. Only then did I realize the man lacked a valise or even a bedroll, so I hoped aloud that he didn't leave his possibles on the Celerity wagon.

"Travel light," he said with ease. "Got all I need."

"I'm Smith Munro." I remembered we'd been too busy for introductions. We kept walking.

"Folks call me Pinto."

"Pinto? Like the horse?"

"Or bean."

"Lots of folks around here ain't partial to that breed of horses," I said.

"I don't care much for that breed of bean," he said, opening the door and letting me go first.

Pa stood waiting, cup of coffee in his hand, Julian right behind him.

Mr. Pinto swept off his hat, and gave Pa and my brother a friendly nod. He introduced himself, and Julian asked if he wanted some coffee, maybe leftover stew.

"Nothing to eat, but coffee sounds invitin'," the stranger said. Maybe he thought our stew had beans in it.

He stood a hat crown's height over Pa and Julian, and I'd guess he still would have towered over them even without those high-heeled boots he wore. Brown corduroy trousers were stuck inside those boots, with a saddle-colored rig around his waist, brass buckle holding up a flapped holster on his right hip, pouch for shot, caps, and powder next to that, and on his left hip, a big Arkansas toothpick in fancy tooled sheath that didn't match the rest of his leather. A Mexican-style jacket of green wool hung unbuttoned on his lanky frame, with a red flannel shirt, and calico bandanna. Hanging from a rawhide thong around his neck, a heavy silver Cross of Lorraine completed his outfit.

His sandy hair looked dirty, greasy, long, and unkempt, but the man had been traveling on Marco Max's Celerity wagon for I didn't know how long, and he sported maybe a week's growth of beard on a pockmarked face highlighted by the coldest green eyes I've ever seen. Now that I could see him in the light, I didn't know quite what to make of him, though calluses covered his hands, and his knuckles were scarred, so he wasn't no stranger to hard work.

"I won't turn a man out," Pa told him. "I won't let any man go hungry from here, but this isn't a hotel. You're 1,051 miles from Fort Smith, 4601/2 from Fort Yuma, and 6 inches to Perdition. Everyone here's an employee of the Overland Mail Company."

"Even the soldier boy?" Pinto stuck his jaw out toward Julian, in his dragoon britches and shirt.

"My son." Pa made the introductions. "Julian will be leaving for his next posting. He's on furlough."

"I see." He took the steaming cup of coffee from Julian, and sipped it. "You seemed short-handed tonight," he said after a moment.

"That why you got off the stage?" Pa asked.

Pinto laughed a little, shaking his head. "Like I told your boy here, I prefer good air in my lungs, and wide open spaces. Wasn't getting that in your mud wagon."

"Where you bound?" That wasn't a real polite question, but Pa didn't appear to be in a friendly mood.

"Texas," he said, not offended. "Home. Rusk County. Been at Vallecito for the past three, four years. But war's coming. Home's the place to be in a time of war."

"Texas pulled out of the Union," I sang out.

"So I heard."

A moment, a long one, too, stretched out as Pinto sipped his coffee, and Pa sized him up. Finally the stranger set the empty cup on the table and hooked his thumbs in his belt on either side of the brass buckle. "Mr. Munro," he said. "I ain't forcin' myself on you. You need a hand . . . like I said, I'm willin' to earn my keep. More'n willin', actually. I'd demand it. Not a man who cares for charity. If you don't want me here, just give the word and I'll light out. Walk to the next station or Franklin if I have to. Walk to Rusk County if need be."

"You'd walk?" Pa said. "After you paid, what, $150 in gold to ride?"

Shrugging, Pinto answered: "Not quite that much, for passage from Vallecito to Gainesville. Like you said, you didn't invite me. Wouldn't be the first bet I've made and lost."

"Giles Hawley is the superintendent," Pa told him. "He hangs his hat in Tucson. He does all the hiring. That means I can't pay you." He wet his lips, and quickly added: "If I let you stay."

"Didn't ask for pay. Coffee's fine. I'll work for found." He turned around and looked down at me, smiling. "Long as it ain't pinto beans."

"You know horses?"

"Worked in a livery in Vallecito. Rode herd for

one of them big Mexican *haciendas* before that. Yeah, I know horses. And I know mules."

"He knowed better. . . ."

"He knew better," Julian corrected me. Now, I didn't like that, not one bit, not getting a school lesson in front of a stranger.

"Well," I said, "he didn't let the mules drink whilst they was . . . while they were hot." I had to stop myself from sticking my tongue out at Julian. I looked at Pa. "And you know how temperamental that big sorrel jack you call Hampton can be."

It's a wonder Hampton ain't died of colic.

"Never cared much for mules." When Pinto said that, I figured Pa would send him packing, but the stranger kept right on talking, and I knew he might stand a chance as Pa's withering gaze slowly faded into something more like amusement. "Till I come to California. Learned a horse is a whole lot more impatient putting a pack saddle on than is a mule. And under that California sun, well, a mule's skin seems to weather better. Ain't so sensitive, a mule's hide. Mind you, I'm Rusk County-born, a Texican, and I don't reckon you'll ever find me raisin' mules. But I've learnt to respect 'em."

That pretty much sold Pa, who told Pinto to bunk with Bartolomé, Fletcher, and Ben Jakes. He told me to show Pinto the way, but the stranger said he could find it all right, and bade us all good night.

"What do you think?" Pa asked Julian after Pinto had left.

My brother shrugged. "He'll do."

Pa refilled his coffee cup. *"Vamos a ver,"* he said in Spanish.

We'll see.

February 10, 1861

We saw tonight with the arrival of the Westbound.
Pinto proved himself a right good hand. Were I Ben
Jakes, I might start fearing for my job. But, no, I
guess Pinto—I called him Mr. Pinto this morning,
because Pa gave me the look, but he shook his head
and told me, and Pa: "There ain't no Mr. to it, Smith.
Pinto is all."—wouldn't take a job even if Pa and Mr.
Hawley offered it. I keep forgetting that Pinto's on
his way to Texas.

It strikes me as I write this that Pinto and Julian
might become enemies, might have to face each other
in battle.

Anyway, Pinto's a good worker, and works real
fast with the teams, and fast is something Pa likes to
see when it comes to changing Overland teams.

This morning, after breakfast, I found Pinto leaning against the stable wall, just looking at the hills
and the yucca. The sky had turned the prettiest blue
you'll ever see, no dust blowing, just a gentle morning breeze, and the cold spell has snapped. February
in Boone County would have me as close to the fire
as I could get. Missouri winters will just freeze the
marrow in your bones, but this is the desert of New
Mexico Territory, and the sun had already started
warming everything.

"That's a view I like," Pinto said as, using a Bar-
low knife, not his big Arkansas toothpick, he cut off
a piece of tobacco and stuck it in his mouth. "Put a
man on that there butte, and ain't nobody going to
come up on him by surprise. Not even an Apache."

"That's Soldier's Farewell Hill," I told him. "The
one you're looking at. The other one, on the other
side of the trail, is what they call Besse Rhodes. And

that one, on the other side of Soldier's Farewell, is named JPB."

"So one's named after some gent with the initials JPB, and the other's after some petticoat." He folded the blade, and slipped the knife into his coat pocket. "Had me an aunt named Bessie, but her last name was Denton."

"No one really knows the story there," I said, showing off my knowledge. "We found a rock up there with the names Besse and Rhodes scratched into it, and underneath them names they'd scratched out USA, so Jules suspects some dragoons named Besse and Rhodes done that, not a. . . ." I grinned despite myself at getting to say the word "petticoat."

"Uhn-huh. Could be. And JPB could be another Yankee handle. How did Soldier's Farewell get its name?"

"All sorts of stories about that." I smiled again, looking for Pa, hoping he might add another tale, but Pa remained inside, talking to Julian and Mr. Fletcher while Bartolomé brought Ben Jakes his breakfast.

"I'd be plumb tickled to hear one." He shifted his tobacco to the other cheek, and spit in the sand.

"Well, one time Pa said this troop of soldiers from Fort Bliss got ambushed by Apaches, and they got whupped on real good, the soldiers did, so they all skedaddled back for Texas, and the Apaches, they laughed and started waving to the soldiers as they run. So it was the Apaches who give this place the name. Soldier's Farewell."

He wiped tobacco juice off his lips. "Well, then," he said, "we might have to name this little knoll by my daddy's farm Soldier's Farewell. If the Yankees try and invade Rusk County."

My smile vanished. I didn't like that image, didn't

like picturing such a fight, one that might involve Julian, and hated myself for thinking of that story among the ten or twelve lies, or maybe one was the truth, that Pa had told me in the past three years or so about the naming of this place. That's because I know Julian wouldn't never have run from a fight like that one. They'd have to kill him. I felt mighty glad when Pinto changed the subject.

"Where's the trail run from here?"

"Right over yonder." I pointed. "It has to cross this draw just before it gets to our station."

"See it. That's why you'd need a sentry up on the hill. That draw's a good place for Apaches to sneak up in. Surprise you. Lot of good hidin' spots in there, 'specially if you're an Injun."

"Apaches have pestered us some," I admitted.

"And beyond the draw?"

"Well, the line runs west to Barney's, about 19. . . ."

"I mean east of here."

"It swings between Soldier's Farewell Hill and Besse Rhodes. You can't make it out from right here, but beyond that is what they call Burro Cienaga. You know what a *cienaga* is?"

"I lived in California," he said. "I savvy quite a bit of that lingo." He snorted. "Wouldn't quite call that a swamp, though, at least it ain't nothing like the swamps we got in East Texas."

"We have some swamps in Missouri, too, but that's what they call it, Burro Cienaga, and it'll hold some water, especially during the monsoons in late summer or when we get all the snow melt in spring. We get our water from the spring back yonder." He knew about that spring, because he had fetched water, but I wanted him to know my part in it, so I told him proudly. "I built the dam."

Ah, fiddlesticks. He acted like he hadn't even heard.

"How far to the *cienaga*?"

"Three miles."

Nodding, he looked again at the little hills, saying absently: "Soldier's Farewell appears taller."

"Yes, sir. But it ain't easy to climb. It's all rocky and steep. I know. I've clumb all three hills."

That sparked his interest. "You're a regular mountain goat, eh?" He tousled my hair the way Pa and Julian sometimes did. "Pretty good view, once you get to the top, I allow?"

"I reckon. But if you're talking about a place for a sentry, I'd choose Besse Rhodes. For one thing, it's easier to climb, and it ain't but maybe 300, 400, no more than 500 feet lower. The thing is, you got hardly a thing blocking your view from up there. A body can look all the way to the Chiricahuas, even past the Organs. You got a clear view of the Overland Trail, too. You can see Cow Springs from up there, all the way to Cooke's Range. Emmett Mills, he's a good friend of Jules's, he works at Cooke's Station. We climbed up Besse Rhodes one time when he was visiting, and he pointed out all the mountain ranges to me."

"And how far's Ojo de la Vaca from here? Julian told me it was 14 miles."

"That's about right," I said. "Once you get out of China Draw, it's a pretty straight trail to here. Marco Max, he can get a team of mules to eat up a lot of countryside in those 14 miles. A 'land-eating gallop,' he calls it."

Pinto spit again. "I rode with him, remember? He'll have his mules at a land-eatin' gallop all the time. Quite the jehu."

"He's my favorite," I admitted.

"Talks like a Yankee," Pinto said, but I didn't say anything to that.

Pa and Julian filed out of the house, and Pinto thanked me for filling him in on the countryside.

I was glad to help.

"Come on, Smith," Pinto said. "Let's go feed some horseflesh."

Again, I felt glad to help.

February 11, 1861

Pinto and Julian rode off this morning to visit the Velásquez family. Well, Julian went to call on Alyvia, and Pinto said he would admire to see some more of this country. Says he might want to settle down here after the Yankee threat in Texas is ended.

I'd wanted to go along, too, but Pa reminded me of chores to be done, piling more stones on the dam, and helping Bartolomé clean the stalls.

They didn't get back from their visit until late tonight.

February 12, 1861

After breakfast, I asked Pinto what he thought about the land he had seen, and he nodded with approval, said it would work mighty fine.

"Work?" I asked. "For what?"

"Hades," he answered, and I laughed.

That Pinto is quite a character.

Same night, or rather morning, after midnight

Eastbound came and went, on time. Stagecoach was chock-full again. Also have news of an uprising among the Apaches at Apache Pass, where that lieutenant named Bascom, who my brother went to the Academy with, has provoked Cochise into war. As if fighting Red Sleeves wasn't bad enough. Upon hearing the news, Julian shook his head and said that sounded just like something Union soldiers would do. Don't know what he meant by that. He's a Union soldier himself.

February 13, 1861

Wednesday. Westbound come tonight, loaded with folks, a bunch of them Texicans, and they all got to jawing with Ben Jakes, who managed to drag his worthless hide out of his bunk for supper, and Pinto, who was helping me feed the horde while the rest, excepting Ben Jakes, of course, changed the teams. Well, the passengers jawed and jawed with us, poured down coffee and ate the slumgullion without complaint. Everything sounded real sociable till one of the travelers said he'd be mighty glad to get to Sacramento before the war started.

"Where you from?" Pinto asked.

"Dallas," the man answered. He wore a plaid sack suit and big silk hat. I'd guess he had to be in his forties, and he wore a single eyepiece, what Julian just told me they call a monocle. I'd never seen one of those before he pulled it out, cleaned it with a handkerchief, set it over his right eye and studied the slumgullion, as if he didn't know what he might find in Pa's concoction.

"They must have run you out of town." Pinto poured a lady a cup of coffee.

Although he never looked back at the man from Dallas and smiled politely at the lady, Pinto didn't try to hide his bitterness. The room turned quiet, but Pinto kept walking around the table, topping off coffee cups, but the man in the silk hat stood up, returning the monocle to his vest pocket.

"What do you mean, sir, by that remark?"

Pinto looked up. "Dallas ain't known to cotton to cowards." He spoke in a matter-of-fact voice. "Nowhere in Texas tolerates cowards."

Puffing out his chest, his face turning redder than Pinto's flannel shirt, the man pushed back his coat and rested his right hand on the butt of a single-shot Derringer. "Are you calling me a coward?"

"You called yourself one," said the Texican, sitting right beside him, a burly man in a tan hat with a brown patch over his left eye and a scar stretching from one cheek across the bridge of his nose to the other.

The insulted man looked away from Pinto, who took that opportunity to place his hand on that big knife on his hip, the flap on his holster preventing him from getting to his pistol in a timely fashion.

"'Twas you who said you wanted to get out of Texas before shootin' commenced." Slurping up a mouthful of slumgullion, the big Texican didn't even bother to look up.

"I . . . you . . . I. . . ." The Dallas man just got redder and redder. "Well." Then he found his nerve. "I don't see either of you bound for Texas to defend her sovereign soil."

Immediately he regretted those words, for the man with the eye patch pushed away his bowl, and stood. He carried a big old Walker Colt belted around his belly, and that took some doing, because a Walker's a horse pistol, meant to be carried on the saddle pommel, and a giant Bowie sheathed on his left hip. The fellow from Dallas had practically called Pinto, and the man with the eye patch, cowards.

The lady gasped, and the Dallas gent didn't look so red any more. He kept getting paler and paler, especially when Mr. Eye Patch said: "You best apologize or I'll blow a hole in your brisket."

Yet it was Pinto who spoke. "It's me who needs to apologize," he said, taking his hand off the hilt of his knife and lifting the coffee pot again. "Should have known better than to provoke some-thin'." He bowed at the lady. "I'm sorry, ma'am." Turning to Mr. Dallas, he spoke softly but firmly. "I withdraw my statement, sir. It's no business of mine what takes you to California."

"War's comin'," Mr. Eye Patch told Pinto. "Mighty soon."

"We'll be ready," Pinto said.

That's when Pa come in, and he frowned mightily at two passengers standing, one of them looking sick, and nobody talking. His eyes landed on Pinto, who wet his lips and went back to pouring coffee.

"Drink up," Pa said. "Coach leaves in less than 5 minutes."

Afterward, I had to explain to Pa and Julian what all had happened. I feared Pa would send Pinto on his way, so I came to his defense, saying how he had stopped bloodshed, had apologized. Don't think Pa liked it none, but he didn't say more on the subject.

Same night, 11 o'clock

About to turn in.

Julian just told me: "You seem to like this Pinto."

"He's all right," I said.

"I wouldn't get close to him, Smith," he said.

"Ain't like I'm replacing you, Jules," I said, with a grin. "You're blood. He ain't. He's just. . . ."

Julian cut me off, repeating what he'd said, but this time it came out more like an order. "Don't get close to him, Brother. He's a killer."

Killer?

February 14, 1861

All day, I've been thinking about what Julian told me last night. Pinto, Bartolomé, and Fletcher are shoeing horses. Pa's scratching out a report to send off to Superintendent Hawley. Ben Jakes is up and about, but not really lending a hand, and I've washed all the dishes. Don't know where Julian took off to, but he saddled up Sweet Ainsley and rode out, probably to court Alyvia. I haven't seen the Velásquezes in a coon's age, seems like.

Killer, Julian called Pinto. Don't know where he came to that conclusion, but it's got me wondering, maybe worrying.

Killer.

Well, it strikes me that Pinto stopped a killing last night. It was Pinto who apologized, who prevented Mr. Eye Patch from likely killing that guy from Dallas, who probably is a coward. Acted like one, if you ask me.

Pinto's all right. I guess what I like about him is he's different. And he's here. Somebody new. I mean, the one good thing about working at Soldier's Farewell is that you get to meet a lot of interesting folks. Schoolteachers and miners and drummers and soldiers and adventurers, people who have lived in the East, people who have seen the Pacific Ocean. You meet them, and they've come from all over the United States, mostly Missouri and California, sure, but all over. However, you don't get to know them. You just meet them, talk to them over their food if it's the Westbound, and if they're going East, you hardly even see them.

Pinto stayed. I don't know how long he'll be here, but he's different, and he's here.

It's coming on three years now that I've been living at Soldier's Farewell. People would come to Boone County, Missouri, and they'd place roots. You'd get to know them. Unless you count the men who work at this station, I haven't gotten to know hardly anyone, excepting the Velásquezes, since we got here, and maybe folks like Emmett Mills and Mr. Barney, but they are not really neighbors, just other employees of the Overland.

So . . . Pinto . . . he's here, he's new, he's different, and he listens to me. Seemed real interested and impressed when I told him all about the draws and such, and the difference between the hills around the station.

That's all. Not like he's my brother or nothing. He's just somebody new and interesting. I don't think he's a killer, though. Not unless you gave him cause.

February 15, 1861

"Killed him?" Pa looked incredulous. "Killed him?"

It's after midnight, the Eastbound is gone, and I'm sitting in the corner, scratching put these words, lessen I forget. Not that I think I could ever forget.

It happened like this.

The Eastbound pulled in right on time, with Marco Max driving, and, while Little Terry jumped down to help us with the team, Marco Max set the brake and climbed down off the stage, too, which he has never done while driving the Eastbound.

"Munro!" he yelled, and Pa, who was fetching the fresh team with Julian and Fletcher, pulled away and headed to him, while Pinto run from the team we were unhitching to give Julian and Fletcher a hand.

"What in blazes is going on?" Pa yelled, and Marco Max just kept walking to him, till he got real close, and they started jawing. Couldn't hear a word they said until Pa bellowed: "Killed him? Killed him?"

Well, that got all our attention. Bartolomé and me looked up, just stopped what we was doing, until Little Terry reminded us of the work to be done. We got back to the harness, but our ears stayed trained on Pa and Marco Max.

Bartolomé asked Little Terry something in Spanish, but the messenger just shrugged, spit out tobacco juice. "Mr. Munro'll tell you about it. Let's get a move on."

So we pulled the team away, and Bartolomé and I led the mules to the stable. I had time to glance over my shoulder, to see Pa and Marco Max still talking as the jehu headed back to the stagecoach and climbed back into the box.

The stage pulled out, and I felt certain sure I wouldn't. . . .

Pa's demanding I quit writing and go to bed. Will have to finish this tomorrow.

February 16, 1861

Back to what all happened last night. I thought Pa wouldn't tell me a thing about who had gotten killed, where, or why, figured he'd just tell me to go to bed, treat me like I was a kid, and then he and Julian and maybe Mr. Fletcher would talk about things. So it struck me like an axe when I walked into the room and Pa fired out hot words:

"What went on the other night on the Westbound, Smith? Between those two passengers? And Pinto?"

I looked around. Pinto wasn't there. Probably had turned in with the rest of the hands. Even Fletcher wasn't inside.

"I. . . ."

"What happened?" Pa roared.

I hadn't done a thing, so I felt scared and a bit angry. I hadn't tried hiding anything from Pa. He hadn't asked about the fight that never come about. Well, I told Pa, and Julian, the truth, how Pinto had called the man in the silk hat a coward, how the guy with the eye patch had done the same, but then how Pinto had done all the apologizing, and things settled down and all.

"Pinto stopped them from killing one another," I said, coming to Pinto's defense.

Pa spit. "Not hardly."

"But he did," I said. "You can ask him."

"I plan to. The guy with the eye patch shot the other one dead when they got to Barney's."

"Killed him?" I couldn't believe it. Sounded just like Pa had when Marco Max spilled the news.

"Killed him." Sagging, Pa sank into his chair and shook his head. "They exchanged some more words after leaving here. The man with the scar and patch kicked him off the stage, right out the door, when they pulled in to Barney's Station, jumped out, drawing his revolver, and shot him twice in the chest."

"Must have been some conversation between those two," Julian said.

With a snarl, Pa slammed his fist on the table. "This ain't funny."

"No, sir," Julian said.

"No, sir," I added, even though I hadn't laughed or cracked a grin.

"The company doesn't like paying customers getting killed," Pa said.

"It happened at Barney's," Julian said. "Not here. It isn't your fault. And it's not Smith's."

It's not Pinto's, either, I started to add, but instead reminded them: "That man, the one from Dallas, he had a Derringer in his waistband. I saw it. He started to pull it on Pinto. So maybe he tried for it, tried to shoot the man with the patch, and that's how come he got killed."

Pa kept quiet, but I don't think he considered anything I said. To him, Mr. Eye Patch had committed murder in cold blood.

"What happened after the shooting?" I asked.

"Took off, the man did, ran south. Other one was dead. Both bullets hit his heart. It was dark. Barney and two others went looking for him come first light, but they couldn't find the trail."

"You should get *Señor* Vee," I said. "He could track down that fellow."

Shaking his head, Pa slowly stood. "Trail's cold by now. Barney can't spare any manhunters, either."

"You can," Julian said, and that stopped Pa and me.

"Put Jakes back to work," my brother said. "He's fine, just lazy. Pinto and I'll scout for that *hombre*."

"Cochise or some other Apache probably has killed him by now," Pa said.

"Did Marco know the man's name? Where he was bound?" Pa shook his head.

"He went south." Julian considered this. "But I don't think he'd run or walk all the way to the border. Probably swing back north. To Burchville and the Pinos Altos mines. That's a good place for anybody to disappear."

"If he knows the territory," Pa said. "Coming from Texas, he might not."

"Maybe the man with the monocle drew his Derringer," I suggested again. "Could be it was self-defense."

"That's for the courts to decide," Pa said. "There's such a thing as the law, even in New Mexico Territory." He gave my brother a look I can't quite describe, like he was trying to figure something out. "What's your interest? Why should you risk your hide going after him? Like you just said, it happened at Barney's, not here. Not our concern."

"I'm a soldier."

Pa's head shook. "Not a military matter."

Julian suddenly grinned. "Then how about this, Pa? It'll give me something different to do. Something interesting."

Silence. Outside, the wind picked up.

"I'll ask Pinto," Julian said, deciding for himself. "We'll ride out at dawn. See if we can track down the man-killer. Bring him back here. Put him on the stage to Mesilla, or take him there ourselves. Let a grand jury sort it out."

Said Pa: "If you find him."

Julian grinned like he'd just been challenged.

"You could ride over to *Señor* Vee's," I said. "He's the best tracker in the territory."

My brother shook his head. "Wouldn't want to inconvenience him," Julian said. "Besides, I learned a few things about tracking while chasing Paiutes."

That's what Julian and Pinto done. Before breakfast, they lit out on two good mules, pulling an extra one, saddled and all, in case they found Mr. Eye Patch, behind them.

Pa just stood there, the wind blowing, just stood and watched as they rode out, till you couldn't see them any more, and then he walked away. He made a beeline for Besse Rhodes, started climbing the hill. When he reached the top, he'd watch the dust trail Julian and Pinto made.

It's noon now, and, though Pinto and Julian must be long out of sight, Pa ain't yet come down.

February 17, 1861

A Sunday. Julian and Pinto haven't come back yet. This morning over breakfast, Pa told me not to worry about them, that Pinto and Julian could take care of themselves, then made me recite a Bible passage before I could eat. "And don't say 'Jesus wept,'" he instructed me. I thought about telling him that I wasn't hungry, and I wasn't, and therefore would not quote the Good Book this morning, but that would have just provoked a whipping. So I spoke from Deuteronomy, mainly because a lady passenger had said this a few days back when I dished her a bowl of slumgullion and wormy hardtack.

" 'Thou shalt not eat any abominable thing.' "

"You commenting on my cooking?" Pa tried to smile, to make me think he wasn't worried, either, but I could see through that plain as day.

Same day, half past 8

Julian still not home. Waiting on the Westbound.

February 18, 1861

No word from Julian, but *Señor* Vee showed up this morning, and rode out after a private talk with Pa. I imagine Pa asked him to go looking for Julian. *Señor* Vee says we can expect a visit from the rest of his family.

I should take time to write some of the news we heard from the passengers last night.

No news about Fort Sumter, but the states that have dissolved the Union—South Carolina, Mississippi, Florida, Alabama, Georgia, Louisiana, and Texas—were meeting in Montgomery, Alabama, to elect a President and write a constitution for the new nation, the Confederate States of America. There were two men from Mississippi on the stage, and there was much talk about who would become President.

Another person, who was from Chambersburg,

Virginia, I think, kept quoting from this newspaper called the *Valley Spirit*.

" 'Is the country to be subjected to the horrors of civil war? We hardly see how that calamity can be averted as things are going.' " He kept on, had most of this story memorized, or at least that's what he said, and the article had been written and published back in December. He kept on talking, until another passenger, and this one sounded like he just arrived from Ireland, he broke out laughing.

"Civil war," he says. "Trust me, lads, there will be nothing civil about the coming war."

One of the men from Mississippi snorted, protesting that the war would be over in six weeks, but the Irishman just looked up, and his face turned sad, and he didn't say a thing, just looked with his cold blue eyes, and the man from Mississippi stared at his coffee cup, and nobody else spoke until Pa come inside and announced the stage was fixing to leave.

February 19, 1861

Before the arrival of the stage, we had a fandango yesterday afternoon. Julian and Pinto rode back, along with *Señor* Vee, just an hour or so after *Señora* Dolores arrived with Tori and Alyvia. We ate *chiles rellenos, frijoles, tortillas*, and *empanadas* stuffed with mincemeat, enough good food that would certainly make Pa's slumgullion, especially as watered down as it has been the past three, four days, seem like something abominable. It was like *Señora* Dolores knew Julian would be coming home, although she couldn't have.

The man with the Eye Patch wasn't with them.

"Any sign of him?" Pa asked while the womenfolk cleared off the table and washed the dishes, which made me mighty happy as I wouldn't have that chore to do later, or then.

"Apaches got him," Pinto answered, and Julian shot him an odd look. Reckon on account of how loud Pinto said it, might have frightened *la señora* and her girls. "We buried him." He sipped his coffee, swallowed, and shook his head. "What was left of him."

Señor Vee crossed himself.

"Well. . . ." Pa smoothed his mustache. "You cut any sign, Alejondro?"

Pa's Mexican friend shook his head, and Julian spoke up.

"We'd buried the *hombre* and were coming back home when we found Mr. Velásquez." A wide grin spread across my brother's face. "Or, I guess I should say, when he found us."

"Where'd you find the Texican?"

Julian and Pinto looked at each other. "South," Julian said uncomfortably. "Past Black Mountain."

"He covered a lot of ground, being afoot," Pa said.

"Yes, sir," Julian and Pinto agreed.

"I thought he'd turn toward the mines," Julian said. "Didn't know the country, I guess."

"Yeah." Pa nodded, but it looked like he hadn't even heard. He just sat, thinking, stroking that big mustache. "Didn't look like some greenhorn, though. Looked like a man who knew how to handle himself." He thought about this some more. "If not striking north for the mines, he should have made his way closer to the Overland Trail, where he'd know he could find some water."

"Good way to get caught," Pinto said.

"Sneak in at night. Draw water from the springs. Hide in the daytime." Pa shook his head. "How'd y'all cut his trail?"

"We didn't," Julian said quickly. "All we saw was the buzzards. Then we found him."

Again, *Señor* Vee crossed himself, and Pa sighed.

"Pa," Julian said. "I'm not sure he walked all the way to Black Mountain. I think the Apaches caught him quickly, maybe the night he killed the fool from Dallas. The Indians were riding for Mexico, and they brought him along, then tortured him, left him for dead. If you want, and if Mr. Velásquez will accompany me, we'll ride back in the morning, see what signs he can find. Maybe we'll learn a better account of what must have happened." He swallowed, and we all waited.

Pa started to speak, but Tori came over and asked if anyone wanted coffee, but we all shook our heads, and she left, disappointed.

"Well?" Julian asked.

"No," Pa said. "No point in that. I'll write a note to Barney and Giles, tell them what you discovered, and I thank you, thank you both, for going after him, giving him a Christian burial." He nodded at *Señor* Vee. "Much obliged, Alejondro. *Mil gracias.*"

"*De nada.*"

"Apaches." Looking off at the hills, Pa went back to fingering his mustache. "Could be more trouble. We'll double the guards."

"They were headin' for Mexico," Pinto said. "I don't think they'll trouble us."

"Maybe. Maybe not." Pa rose. "Still, just to be safe, we'll double the guards. Alejondro, you might want to spend the night here, with your family. In case Apaches are here. The women can sleep inside. The boys and me can bed down elsewhere."

"Your hospitality is much appreciated, *mi amigo*," *Señor* Vee began, and the way he looked over his shoulder, I knew he would decline Pa's offer. "But I want to go to my own home. This place. . . ." He stopped. Alyvia, Tori, and his wife had returned, smiling, and we all painted on our faces the most awful-looking smiles anyone has ever seen.

They left—they never wanted to be here of nights— and, true to his word, Pa doubled the guards. Not that he'd let me lend a hand.

February 20, 1861

Pa sent his report on the finding and burial of Mr. Eye Patch on the Westbound tonight, and he warned us not to mention the Apaches to any of the passengers. Guards are still doubled.

Spent this morning with Julian, like I was in school, going over the *Reader* and writing and talking in good English. He says my spelling's really good, and my construction and grammar keep getting better but still need some work.

February 21, 1861

More schooling from Julian. I'm starting to wish he'd leave for his new posting.

February 22, 1861

This morning, Julian saddled Sweet Ainsley and said he was going to ride over to the Velásquez place, just to make sure they were all right.

"Take Smith with you," Pa said.

That shocked me almost as much as it did Julian.

"I don't know," Julian said. "With the Apaches. . . ."

"Take him. Should be all right. Like Pinto said, those Indians are most likely in Mexico by now. And your brother has been cooped up here too long. Do him some good to see the country." I detected a twinkle in Pa's eyes. "And maybe a chaperone for you and Miss Alyvia."

"Pa!" Julian protested, and I started laughing real hard until Pa added something.

"Maybe your brother would like to court Victoria."

"Pa!" I shouted, and Julian got a turn at laughing.

Will have to finish this in the morning. Anyway, I'm back home, but tuckered out. Covered a lot of ground in one day.

February 23, 1861

Need to write about what happened. Julian told me not to mention a word to Pa, and that's fine, but I guess I can write about it. That's what this diary is for.

It struck me as mighty peculiar. Well, let me write just the way it happened.

Julian and I were riding, side-by-side, through this grove of yuccas, when, from out of nowhere, this man appeared. One second there was nothing but a bunch of desert, and in the time I blinked, I found myself staring at a cruel-looking individual blocking our trail.

"Apache!" I screamed, and started to tear out of this country, but Julian reached over and grabbed my reins.

"Smith!" he yelled. "It's all right. He's a friend."

I didn't hear him, not at first, must have gone a little crazy with fear, but Julian remained calm.

"Friend?" I looked at my brother, my chest heaving, my heart pounding like it might explode, and then looked again at the silent figure between the tall yuccas.

He wore Apache moccasins and duck trousers, a Mexican serape over a muslin shirt, straw hat, and a big .45 belted in a yellow sash. What I noticed most, however, were the long hair, flowing past his shoulders, and eyes, blacker that a raven's.

"He's a. . . ."

"He's a half-breed," Julian said. I couldn't see how he could talk so calm. "Scout for the Army. Trust me, Smith, he helped us when I was in the dragoons, scouted for us when we went after the Paiutes."

My lips still trembling, I made myself calm down, and the mean-looking *hombre* smiled.

"Thought . . . he . . . soil . . . britches." He spoke in a guttural voice, deep, broken, mean. He might have thought he was funny, but I found nothing comical, although I had to check myself, make sure I hadn't wet my pants or done something worse.

"What's his name?" I asked Julian.

"Nicanor," the half-breed said, no longer smiling. "But you call me Breed. Most do. I'm not insulted by the name."

"What's he doing here?" I blurted out at Julian. I didn't understand anything.

"I'm here," Breed said with some irritation. "Ask me."

I made myself look at him, swallowed down the fear in my throat, waited for my stomach to settle. Slowly Julian released the reins, and rested his hands on the horn of his saddle.

"What . . . ?" I swallowed again. "What . . . ?" I made myself sound friendly, casual. "What brings you here, Breed?"

The smile returned, revealing a couple of gold front teeth, and Breed turned, pointing down the road. "Horses," he answered.

"¿Caballos?" Señor Vee scratched his head, staring at the horses Breed had in a string, behind the paint horse he rode.

"That's right," Julian answered. "We just want to keep our horses here. For two, maybe three days."

"Yo no entiendo." He looked past my brother, past me, and his face locked on the hard figure of Breed.

"It's like this, Mr. Velásquez," Julian said. "I rode with Breed with the 1st Dragoons. He's a good man, and he knows horses, *caballos. Muy bien.* We want to raise horses. Sell them to the Army."

Looking at the horses, I frowned. So did *Señor* Vee. Julian glanced over his shoulder, realized what bothered us, and grinned. "Yes, they're geldings. But that's what the dragoons want. The Army doesn't care to mix stallions with mares. Hard to form regular lines in battle. We'll raise horses, or buy geldings, break them, sell them to the dragoons. It's a business. Uh . . . *negocios.*"

"Sí." Señor Vee stepped back.

"Sir," Julian said, "you know my father. He's a jackman. Mules are his life. *Mulas*. Now, do you think he'd let me keep a bunch of rangy geldings with his jennies and jacks, his horses and donkeys? Do you know what . . . how much Cain he'd raise if he found out his oldest son wanted to raise horses, *caballos*, in Texas, and sell them to the Army?"

I think Julian was talking to me, as much as he was to *Señor* Vee, when he said that. He removed his hat, and brushed bangs out of his eyes. He was almost sweating, so I could picture how nervous he would be if he had to explain all this to Pa.

"Two or three days," Julian said. "Then I'll be leaving for my next posting. . . ."

The rest of his words faded. Julian had said nothing about leaving. In two or three days. Hardly any time at all. My heart sank.

"*Días. Dos o tres*," Julian said. "Then they'll be gone. *Deja*."

Breed spoke up, in Spanish, doing a better job of it than my brother had done, and at last *Señor* Vee understood, because he grinned a great big one, and said something, his head bobbing. He knew exactly what my father would say about Julian's choice in horseflesh.

"And I have to ask you," Julian said, but, again, he directed his words at both me and Pa's Mexican *amigo*. "Please, *por favor*, say nothing of these horses to my father."

Señor Vee nodded. "Your secret is safe with me. They can stay here two or three days."

"Breed can stay," Julian said. "I mean, with your permission. Uh, *con . . . su . . . permiso*. He'll tend the horses." Julian gestured at Breed.

"*Durante dos o tres días*," *Señor* Vee repeated, but

he didn't sound like he'd enjoy having Breed around.
I don't blame him.

I didn't speak much on the way home.

"You won't mention the horses to Pa, will you,
Smith?" he asked.

I shook my head.

"Sorry Breed scared you, Smith. He looks mean,
but. . . ."

The hoofs of the mules clopped along the rocks.
In the distance, I could see the small peaks. Soldier's
Farewell. Julian was leaving.

"Hey." Julian pointed to a cloud. "What does that
one remind you of?"

"You're leaving," I blurted out. Petulant. Couldn't
help it.

He reined in Sweet Ainsley, let out a heavy sigh,
and, when I didn't stop, he barked out an order. I
pulled Ivanhoe to a halt, looked back at my brother.

"You knew I wouldn't be here forever, Smith." He
pointed east. "I'm on furlough. You know that. The
war's coming. Pa can deny it all he wants, but that
won't stop it. I'm obliged to fight. I have to fight. It's
called duty."

Well, now, I couldn't stop the tears once Julian
said all that, as much as I tried, as much as I wanted
to act like a man in front of my brother, a second
lieutenant with the 1st United States Dragoons.
Criminy, the dam up and busted wide open, and
suddenly I found myself bawling, gripping the
saddle horn till my knuckles turned white. Ashamed,
I felt, and more that a bit scared, not about the half-
breed we had left at the Velásquez place, but for my
brother, and the approaching war.

"I don't want you to get killed, Jules!" I choked

out when he rode up to me, put his arm around my shoulder, hugging me close, almost pulling me off my mule.

"Mark my words, Innis Smith Munro," he whispered. "I won't get killed. I promise you that."

He waited until I regained some composure, and then, dabbing the tears and wiping the dirt off my streaked face with his bandanna, he warmed me with his smile. "There," he said at last. "You feeling better?"

Best answer I could manage was a feeble nod.

"Let's get back home." He retied the bandanna around his neck. "And, please, little Brother, don't mention those horses to Pa. He'd want to see them, then spend the next three days telling me what a poor lot they are. That's one fight I'm not ready for. That's one fight I'd never win."

February 24, 1861

Plenty to write about. Eastbound brings news of Jefferson Davis, who Pa knew back in Mississippi, a report about President Lincoln, and another—if you can believe this—gentleman traveler, who got off after buying a ticket from Tucson to Soldier's Farewell. Never heard of anyone buying a ticket for here, but he says he plans on joining some friends from Mesilla and heading to Burchville to try his hand at mining. They know to meet him here in a few days and continue the journey north.

His name is J.T. Cassady, and he speaks in a soft accent, although Pa says he sounds like his mouth is filled with cornbread and molasses. He has agreed to pay his way and sleep in the stable, and if he has enough gold to pay what Pa charges for meals, he doesn't need to be going to the Pinos Altos mines because he must already be rich.

He is a middle-aged fellow, bald on the top of his head, the rest of his hair dark and flecked with gray, but I ain't got no idea how old he is. Could be 40. Could be 60. A bit on the heavy side, dressed in a plaid sack suit, and wearing a gray bell-crown hat. Light brown eyes, which I heard Pa call rheumy, and lugging around a battered old carpetbag.

Anyway, he's here. Don't know for how long. Tends to keep out of our way and just walk around the yard, although Pa has told him not to wander too far from the buildings unless he wants to wind up in the hands of the Apaches. We haven't seen sign of Indians of late, but it pays to be careful at Soldier's Farewell.

Now, I should write about Lincoln and Davis. News seems to be spreading a lot faster these days. I reckon more folks are interested in what's happening, how close we're getting to the war back East.

Well, the Union President will be inaugurated next month, in just a few days. I reckon Mr. Lincoln is in Washington City already, as he left Springfield, Illinois, on February 11, but the big news comes from Montgomery, Alabama, where Jefferson Davis has been selected as President of the new Confederate States of America. That comes as a surprise to most, at least according to the jehu, Big Terry, and that J.T. Cassady gent, who says he has family in Mobile, which he tells me is on the Gulf of Mexico in Alabama.

What I noticed, reading the paper, is that North Carolina sent representatives to Montgomery with the rest of the states of the new nation, but

North Carolina hasn't dissolved the Union yet. I pointed that out to Julian, but it was Mr. Cassady who spoke on the subject. "A matter of time," he said in that slow drawl. "A matter of time. Those Tarheels will soon join our just and righteous cause."

I guess it's all over. The Union, I mean. When I told Pa that, he didn't answer me, just sighed and walked outside, where I saw him standing at the stable, looking at our battered old flag, fluttering in the wind.

Over. Really over. At least, that's what the Mesilla *Times* is reporting. The headline in the latest paper declared:

IT IS FINISHED

Big Terry and Donnie Oh, the conductor, brought the paper on the stage, and gave it to Pa, and Julian suggested this morning after breakfast that I copy some of the story into my diary. Good to practice writing, he said. So this is from the *Times*, which, as I've written a while back, Emmett Mills doesn't think highly of, but it is news, important news, so here it is:

The deed has been done. We breathe deeper and freer for it. The Union is dead. It was a great, a glorious fabric; but its timbers had rotted at the heart.

I was rereading that passage aloud when Pa come in from the stables, and he frowned, spit, and suggested I take that newspaper to the privy, where it belongs.

"Smith's just practicing reading and writing," Julian told him.

"He'd do better practicing on something other than that trash," Pa fired back, turned, and walked outside. I guess he doesn't think much of the newspaper, same as Emmett Mills.

Same day, 5 o'clock

I just came in from the stables, and found Pa sitting at the table, reading the *Times.* I didn't say anything to him, just came to my bunk to write this down. He looked mighty interested in the writing, especially seeing how he told Julian it was trash earlier today.

February 25, 1861

Waiting for Julian to tell Pa that he's leaving. It must be tomorrow. I wonder why he ain't mentioned it. Today, he rode off after breakfast on Sweet Ainsley to see Alyvia, but I know he also went to check on his geldings, and Breed. Pinto asked if he could ride out, too, but not with my brother. He wanted to ride along the trail for a bit, and Pa let him. Ain't seen much of Mr. Cassady today. No sign of those men who he's supposed to meet here. Hope the Apaches haven't gotten them.

Same day, half past 9 o'clock

Julian rode back around suppertime, said he wasn't hungry, and after I went out to fetch a bucket of water from the spring, I come back inside and found him reading this diary.

That riled me some, and Julian slammed the cover shut.

"I'm examining your grammar, Smith," he said. "You're getting the hang of it, but you need to remember that there is no such word as ain't."

"Well, you ain't supposed to read another person's diaries. That's what Ma told Pa long ago." I felt madder than a scorpion. "'A diary is for the person writing in it.' That's what Ma said. So I don't think you need to be reading about my thoughts, wishes." I had to think about what all Pa had told me when I first got this book. "Hopes," I added. "Dreams."

Julian's face revealed how angry he was when I first started snapping at him, but it softened when I mentioned Ma, and he gently handed me the book. "You're right, little Brother," he said. "I apologize."

I snatched it from his hand, sat down in my corner. "When you telling Pa you're leaving?" I asked. That's really what kept festering, not the fact that he had read my innermost thoughts.

"Tomorrow," he replied softly. "Maybe the day after. Thanks for not telling him about that, Smith. Or about the horses at Mr. Velásquez's place."

"You tell Alyvia that you're going?"

His head shook, and he stared at his stocking feet. "I haven't told anyone. Only you. And Alyvia's father, of course."

I handed him back the diary. "You can read it," I told him. "I don't really mind. I don't have many hopes and dreams."

He shook his head. "You should. A boy your age should be filled with hopes and dreams." He let out a little laugh. "Why, I remember when I was your age. I had big plans and dreams. I was. . . . Well, it doesn't matter about me and those long ago dreams."

"You got any dreams now?" Prying, I was, trying to see if he planned on marrying Alyvia, but Julian didn't answer. Just rolled into his bed—my bed that he had been borrowing all this time—and said he was tuckered out.

He's snoring now. Almost as loud as Pa.

February 26, 1861

Big excitement when the Eastbound arrived this morning right on time.

Excitement at first, I mean. Then trouble. Bad trouble.

It all started when three passengers got off as soon as the stagecoach pulled to a stop, one from inside the Celerity and the other two climbing down from the top.

Before Pa could yell at them, the jehu said this was their destination, and Pa shouted that Soldier's Farewell was no boarding house.

"Ve vill not inconvenience you very long, *Herr* Munro," said the one who had been inside the coach. "Uh . . . ve vill not be here long." He clicked his boot heels and bowed slightly. "Captain Ulf Beckenbauer, 6th United States Infantry. At your service!"

He pointed a redwood staff, which he had carried under his left armpit, at the two other men, who, just from how they stood, I had already determined to be soldiers.

"Lieutenant Day *und* Sergeant Scott, of the dragoons."

It was one of those associates who grabbed my attention when he asked Pa: "Is Julian here, sir?"

* * *

Lieutenant Richardson Day must have been the tallest man I'd ever met, with light blue eyes and wavy blond hair, and dressed in the uniform of the 1st U.S. Dragoons, so I figured he had fought with Julian against the Paiutes. The other fellow, Sergeant Lucas Scott, resembled a bear, with a thick black beard and a chest shaped like a water barrel, and about as solid as one, too. The strip of black fur on the headband of his forage cap made me think even more of a bear when I looked at him.

Captain Beckenbauer was a big man, too, silver hair and mustache painted with brown streaks, and a left hand that I tried not to stare at . . . only couldn't help myself. It looked like a vine that had withered and turned black after a killing frost, but I wouldn't say that bad hand made the captain weak. Nothing like that at all. He appeared as tough as Lieutenant Day looked tall.

"What brings you out this way?" Pa asked as we poured them coffee in our little abode after the stagecoach left.

Silently Julian stood back in the corner. I figured he would be glad to see some pals of his from Fort Tejon, but he looked to be off his feed. Oh, he had shaken their hands and all, outside, after hearing Lieutenant Day ask about him, and again, inside, when we came in out of the chill, but he wasn't treating these soldiers as friends. To me, he seemed to study our visitors with a bit of anxiety.

The big German made a face as he tested Pa's coffee, and nodded at Richardson Day, so the tall lieutenant did the answering.

"Captain Beckenbauer has been ordered to intercept known Southern sympathizers. Sergeant Scott and I are on detached service with him."

"You expect to find sympathizers at Soldier's Farewell?" Pa asked.

Almost immediately I thought about Ben Jakes shooting off his mouth about Texas and fighting Union soldiers, and silently I cursed him, thinking his wild talk had been reported by some of the Overland passengers, and now they had sent the Army to arrest all of us.

Lieutenant Day looked uncomfortable.

"It's. . . ." He stared past Pa and at Julian. "I figured you would have joined the Rebels back in Carolina by now, Jules." Hearing this, Pa and I both whirled, barely catching Day's following words. "Hoped that's where you'd be, anyhow. Not here."

"Rebels!" Pa roared. He started for Julian, stopped, spun back to stare at the soldiers.

Day dropped his head, muttered something underneath his breath, and then looked back up, his face pale, frustrated, confused. "I'm sorry, Jules," he said hoarsely. "I thought your father knew."

"Knew what?" Pa asked, but he knew already. So did I. We didn't need the big German to answer.

"*Herr* Munro is . . . a traitor."

"Captain." Lieutenant Day straightened. "There's no cause for that. Jules is doing what he thinks is right. So have a lot of other officers."

"*Ja, ja, ja.* Und you threw a party in his honor ven he resigned. Bid fond farewell. Shake hands, pour champagne. Till ve meet on the battlefield. I, however, would not toast this man, nor any of his ilk."

The captain spit coffee onto the floor, flung the tin cup rudely on the table, and stared at my brother with hatred filling his eyes. "A traitor," he said again.

"I'm no traitor," Julian said. "I'm doing my duty.

To my home." He stood tall now, my brother, and he walked up to Pa. "I resigned my commission, Pa. I guess I should have told you. I'm bound for South Carolina. Home. To defend my home, my people."

"Your home's here," Pa told him. "Or Missouri."

"No, sir. I was born in South Carolina."

"Your. . . ."

"Pa, I'm Carolina-born. I grew up in Mississippi. That makes me Southern. Even Missouri's likely to pull out of the Union."

"Southron, as they say." The captain spoke with a quiet bitterness. "Traitor. Coward."

For a moment there, I figured Pa would knock down Julian, but when the German kept saying that, calling my brother a traitor, then a coward, Pa practically tore the captain's head off. He spun, rammed a fist into the soldier's nose, slammed the officer back against the wall. The redwood stick dropped from underneath the captain's arm and rattled on the floor. "Shut up, Mr.," Pa said tightly, and, when the sergeant's hand dropped for his holstered pistol, Pa warned him. "Touch that pistol, Sergeant, and I'll kill you."

I stood there, frozen. Couldn't move. Couldn't say a thing. Not even sure I could breathe.

"Leave it be, Sergeant Scott." Lieutenant Day remained the only calm person inside.

"This is my home," Pa told the soldiers. "And this is a private matter between me and my oldest son. You'll leave us alone for a few minutes."

"*Nein*. Not possible." The captain pressed a handkerchief to his nose.

I'll say one thing for that German. Angry as he was, embarrassed, bleeding, he kept himself from losing control, from starting a fight that would lead to a whole lot more bloodshed, and I thought he would do just that for a while there.

"I could have you arrested, *Herr* Munro." He spoke tightly. "Put you in irons." Trembling with rage, the captain started to say something, maybe issue an order to that effect, but he reined himself in, examined his handkerchief, and nodded at the sergeant to pick up his redwood staff.

"I vill forget this," Beckenbauer said when he had the big stick back under his arm, and the handkerchief under his nose. "But if you touch me again, ve vill meet on the field of honor."

"Captain," Lieutenant Day pleaded.

"Lieutenant Day," the German said. "Remember *your* duty."

The tall lieutenant let out a long sigh. "A Southern sympathizer named J.T. Cassady left Tucson. He bought a ticket on the Overland to Soldier's Farewell."

"He's here." Suddenly Pa looked troubled. Concern filled his soft voice, and Pa, when riled, usually didn't speak quiet at all.

"Our orders are to detain him," Day said. "Stop him."

"And protect the payroll," the German said, anger rising again. He thrust the bloody piece of cotton at Julian. "That he plans to rob!"

I should point out that as I write these words, I'm sitting against the wall with Pa and the others. Prisoners. It's like one of those dreams I've written about before, where you wake up and aren't sure if what happened is real or not, but I know. This is no dream. I'm awake. Sitting here, a prisoner in my own home. Writing . . . and waiting. Starting to hate my brother. That German captain, he's dead. They're making Bartolomé and Mr. Fletcher bury him now that it's daylight.

This is what happened.

"Payroll?" Pa glanced over his shoulder at Julian, then turned back to the soldiers. "What are you talking about? What payroll?"

"Army payroll," Lieutenant Day said. "For Fort Tejon. It's coming on the Overland stage."

Pa shook his head. "You're loco. The Overland carries passengers and regular mail only. We don't ship payrolls. It's not allowed. Never has been since Mr. Butterfield started this enterprise."

"That's true." Beckenbauer examined his handkerchief, realized his nose had stopped bleeding, and tossed it beside the coffee cup. He nodded at Lieutenant Day, who sighed and started talking, never taking his eyes off my brother.

"Colonel Dawson, our commanding officer at Fort Tejon, received reports from Tucson of a plan to rob the next payroll shipment. Through communication with Jefferson Barracks, it was decided that the next payroll wagon would be armed, not with money, but guards, so if the bandits tried to hit us, they would be in for a surprise. In the meantime, three couriers, in civilian clothing, would carry the payroll on the Overland, in money belts and in their grips. No one at Wells, Fargo, and Company would know of this."

"*Und* no one did," the German said in a harsh whisper. "But him." He pointed the staff at Julian.

"Well," Lieutenant Day said, "Colonel Dawson knew, as did his adjutant, a couple of others at Fort Tejon, and those involved at Jefferson Barracks. But, yes, Julian knew, because of his duties as commissary of subsistence. The problem is, Colonel Dawson and the others have not resigned, are not joining the Confederacy."

"Traitor," the German said again, and I started for him, started to tell him to quit calling my brother that, but Julian pulled me back, and he went after the captain himself, jerking the staff from the big fellow's hand and flinging it across the room.

"Traitor!" He pointed a finger in the captain's face. "You're the traitor, Beckenbauer! You and those other high-and-mighty, holier-than-thou fools blinded by the North's treachery and deceit. You've broken your promises, your vows. The Army in California is no longer protecting the citizens. What right have you to stop men from leaving California and the territories simply because they feel the South's cause is just?" Julian swung his outstretched arm at Day. "And you, Rich? Are you going to arrest your own brother? You told me yourself how Kenny said he would resign his commission, no matter what Kentucky did, and join the Confederate army. You want to ride up to Cantonment Burgwin, stop him, maybe put him in manacles? Or kill him?"

For a moment, no one spoke, but then Pa asked Julian: "You'd fire on the flag of the United States?" Laughing, without humor, Pa shook his head. "That's like spitting in my face, Julian. I always figured a man could trust his sons, could depend on them. I. . . ."

"Don't start on that, Pa." Julian now stood face to face with my father, and I feared they might come to blows. "I remember you saying umpteen times, how a Scot from Boone County by way of South Carolina and Mississippi could depend on his sons. Southern states, Pa. Southern! What do you want me to do?

Fight the friends and family we had back in Camden and Port Gibson? Fight Ma's relations?" He thrust his arm at the captain. "Fight for him? *Him?* They're arresting men just for what they believe in. They're forgetting what they taught me at the Academy, about *habeas corpus,* about the principles our nation was founded on. It's like the editor wrote in the *Times.* 'The Union is dead . . . its timbers had rotted at the heart.' "

"Your duty. . . ."

"Duty?" Julian shook his head. His eyes were wild, tears welling but blocked from falling by my brother's iron will. "You told me before I left for the Academy about duty, about honor, but I think I left all that at Fort Tejon. We went after those Paiutes, Pa, because Captain Carleton said they had killed some settlers. But those Indians had nothing to do with those killings, Pa. Carleton knew that. Colonel Dawson knew it. We all knew it, but we still pursued the Paiutes. We killed a lot of them. For what? Nothing. Nothing but glory for Dawson and Carleton. Because nobody cares if an Indian is innocent. You want me to fight for that? Or maybe do what George Bascom has done at Apache Pass? Cochise was at peace with us before Bascom started a war. For nothing! That's Union duty for you. Yankee duty. I believe in the Confederacy, Pa. I won't fire on the neighbors we had in Camden and Port Gibson. Or Boone County. That's where my duty belongs. I'm going to South Carolina. I'm going to join Wade Hampton. I'm. . . ."

"Wade Hampton?" Pa fired back. "Son, the last I heard, my dear friend was a senator for the United States."

"He'll resign," Julian argued. "Same as your other

dear friend, Jeff Davis. President Davis! Wade Hampton will fight for Carolina. You know that better than anyone. His loyalty is to South Carolina. Same as mine!"

"All right!" Pa's roar sounded like a cannon, so loud, so violent, Julian had to take a couple of fearful steps back. "If that's what you believe in, fight. Get yourself killed for all I care. But there is no war. Not yet. God willing, it won't come to that, and it won't come here. No shots have been fired. Certainly not at Soldier's Farewell. So you tell me, Julian, and you look me in the eye. You tell me that this German and your lieutenant pal are wrong. Dead wrong. You tell me that you know nothing about robbing an Army payroll. Because unless there's war, that ain't a military action. That's a bunch of bandits stealing. That won't get you any medals. It'll get you hung."

We waited.

"Tell me!" Pa trembled with rage. No, I guess he was fearful, too, just like Julian. Just like me.

Julian swallowed, and stepped away. He couldn't even look at Pa. "Mr. Cassady says the South needs that money."

I barely heard him.

Now, I've always thought of Pa as . . . I don't know, a mountain, bigger than Besse Rhodes or Soldier's Farewell, bigger than anything, but when Julian said that, just above a whisper, and his words registered, well, I thought Pa would charge him, spin Julian around, knock teeth down his throat, but, instead, Pa's shoulders sagged something awful, and when he turned, I could see just how pale his face had turned. He walked to the corner of the room, away from the rest of us, and he just stood there, finally holding out his right hand and leaning against that wall for support.

"Vell," Captain Beckenbauer said. "It is done. If you vill direct us to *Herr* Cassady, ve shall arrest him *und* your son. Vere is the other conspirator?"

The door swung open, and I heard that Southern voice say—"Here I am, boys."—and saw the muzzle flash in the darkness, the belching white smoke, heard the deafening report of the pistol, heard the German grunt, and, turning, I saw him just crumple, letting out a short groan.

Sergeant Scott tried to catch him, but couldn't reach him in time, and then he reacted to the gunshot, tried to draw his pistol, but two men had walked inside, and that J.T. Cassady fellow, who wasn't even holding a gun, warned the sergeant not to be foolish. I almost threw up when I realized who the second man was, the one who had pulled the trigger, for that pistol was in his hand.

"Shuck the sidearms, boys," Pinto said, thumbing back the hammer. "Or join your Yankee captain."

Beckenbauer died directly. After Lieutenant Day and Sergeant Scott unbuckled their belts, they knelt beside the big German, rolled him over onto his back, and lifted his head. "I am killed," he whispered, and, just like that, he died.

I'd never seen a dead man before. Well, not dead like that. I think Pa and Julian had taken me to wakes and funerals back in Missouri, but I can't really remember those, and, sure, Apaches had killed folks all across New Mexico Territory, and white men had done their share of killing, but I hadn't witnessed those, just heard the stories from Pa, *Señor* Vee, and others. Beckenbauer, though, he was shot, shot without warning. I didn't like the German at all, but I sure didn't want to see him murdered.

"You didn't have to kill him," Julian snapped, and Pinto shrugged.

Julian had warned me about Pinto, told me he was a killer. I hadn't believed him.

Noise came from behind them, and Pinto and Cassady stepped aside, and Fletcher, Ben Jakes, and Bartolomé walked inside, followed by another gent that took me a little while to recognize. Then it hit me. He was the man from the stagecoach, the big Texican who had killed the dude from Dallas over at Barney's Station. Apaches hadn't killed him at all. Julian had lied. Lied to me. Lied to Pa.

"You boys grab a seat against the wall there," Cassady said. "You, too, Munro," he told Pa. "I want you-all sittin'. You Yankees do the same. There's nothing you can do for your captain." He looked at the big Texican. "Howell, you and Pinto watch 'em. If they move, let 'em join the captain." Smiling, he ran his hand over his bald head. "Gentleman, please, do not try anything stupid. We'll be together for a little while, waitin' for the Westbound stage, then we shall take our leave. This is for the Confederate States of America."

"I knowed it!" yelled Ben Jakes, wincing from the pain in his ribs. "I'm a Texican myself, by grab. You need any help, just let me know. Always willin' to join a fit for Texas, yes, sir!"

Cassady shot a glance at Pinto. "He's all right," Pinto said. "Full of wind, but he'll do."

"We could use another hand," said the murdering Texican, Howell.

Cassady's head bobbed just slightly. "Very well. Mr.?"

"Jakes. Ben Jakes." He climbed to his feet.

"Very well, Mr. Jakes. Fetch the sergeant's pistol yonder, and welcome to the Southern cause. You stand guard here with Howell. Pinto, come with me. We'll wait outside, consider our options."

"What about him?" Julian pointed at the dead captain.

"We'll bury him come dawn," Cassady said. "In the meantime, have your brother fix us some coffee and food. Something, I dare say, better than that awful slumgullion your father subjects his guests to."

It's dawn now. I'm writing in this book, which has provoked the man named Howell.

"What's he doin', writin' words all this time?" the ugly, one-eyed Texican said a moment ago.

"Leave him be," Julian said. My brother wouldn't look at Pa, wouldn't look at me. He won't even look at Lieutenant Day or Sergeant Scott.

I wonder if they'll kill us after it's all done. Wonder if I'm writing these words for nothing. If they kill us, if they don't burn this book, then whoever finds this diary should know that my father, me, and the Overland hands were shot down in cold blood by the following men:

Ben Jakes.
Pinto.
Howell.
J.T. Cassady.

Julian Munro. That captain was right. He is a traitor.

I have described these men in earlier pages in my

diary. Pretty accurate descriptions. We also have an ambrotype of Julian, before he grew his mustache. I hope *Señor* Vee doesn't find this. He doesn't read or write English and. . . .

The Velásquez family. Oh, Lord, Breed. The half-breed named Nicanor. He's part of the gang of robbers and murderers, too. Let me add him to the list of men you should go looking for. Find my description of him.

I hope, I pray they do not harm Tori, or her sister, her parents.

I'm such a fool.

I should have known. Maybe I did know, just didn't want to believe it. Julian wouldn't let Breed kill Alyvia. Would he? But Julian's here, just sitting there, sipping his coffee, and he didn't stop Pinto from killing Captain Beckenbauer.

Pinto and Ben Jakes are outside, making Bartolomé and Mr. Fletcher dig a grave and bury the German soldier. The rest of us remain inside.

Bartolomé and Mr. Fletcher are back. They didn't say anything, just came in and sat down. Nobody talks much. Not sure what time it is.

A few minutes ago, I heard a horse whinny, followed by talking just outside the door. My heart sank when the door opened and in walked Breed, followed by Pinto.

Is Tori still alive? She's always tormenting me, but I guess, deep down, I really like her, and you won't find better people in all New Mexico Territory than her folks. Her sister's real nice, too.

Cassady came storming through the door a short while later while Breed helped himself to coffee.

"You were supposed to wait for us!" Cassady yelled, but Breed merely shrugged.

"I got tired of waiting, *amigo*," Breed said.

"I don't care how boring you think it is."

"The horses are safe. They'll be there."

"They had better be!"

"*Mi amigo*, don't you trust me?" Breed's grin showed his gold teeth.

"I think it's you who don't trust us," Cassady said angrily.

Breed shrugged. "I want to be certain."

"Then finish your coffee, Breed, and keep an eye on things from the top of the hill outside. Climb up the tallest one."

Pinto shook his head. "No, head up the other one, Breed, the one they call Besse Rhodes. You got a clear view of the whole country from up there, ain't that right, Smith?"

I didn't say anything, but Pinto's laughter as he walked out the door with Breed made me angry, real angry.

"The family?" Julian asked before they got through the door. "Mr. Vel- . . . where you were staying?"

I noticed how he stopped himself from mentioning *Señor* Vee's name, so he doesn't want the rest of us to know where those horses are. That should bring me some relief. That means my brother doesn't plan on killing us after they rob the stage.

Breed grinned. "Today he went hunting. He promised to be back by tomorrow. He trust you, *amigo*." He laughed wickedly then. "No one has harmed his adorable daughters, or his wife." He shook his head, and said: "Her health is good. *Muy bien*. They all fine."

"You better be telling the truth," Julian said, but he was talking to a closed door.

* * *

Must be around noon now, maybe after. My fingers are getting cramped from writing all this down. That's all I can do at the moment.

Writing and waiting.

And hating my brother. Hating myself, too, for being so blind, so stupid, so trusting.

Same day, middle part of the afternoon

They made me fix them all some dinner, more coffee and what's left of the stew. They haven't fed us a thing, not even offered us water, not that I'm hungry. Not even thirsty. The door's open, and Ben Jakes is leaning against the wall just outside, slurping his coffee, watching us, then looking out toward the trail. Wish I had poisoned the coffee, but I wouldn't know how.

Pinto, Howell, and Cassady are sitting where we typically feed the Westbound passengers. I guess Breed remains up on top of Besse Rhodes. Julian's at the table with his 1847 musketoon and a bowl of stew, but he's not eating. He seems distant. Must be his conscience eating at his gut.

No, I reckon not. My brother has no conscience. No soul. Certainly no honor.

The stage isn't due till tomorrow evening. Maybe we can get out of here before then. But how?

I want to ask Pa, but he's just sitting there. He doesn't bring to mind a great mountain of granite any more. He looks, well, I don't know . . . broken? Whipped?

It's all Julian's doing!

When those brigands finished eating, they started for the door, J.T. Cassady picking his teeth with a sliver he'd carved off the table—our table—with a folding knife. When a big gust of wind come along, he heard the flag popping, and he shook his head and spit through the doorway.

"That flag sickens me to my soul," he said. "Old Glory. There's nothin' glorious about that flag any more. Take it down, Pinto. Take it down. It's such a ragged thing anyway. Take it down, I say, and burn it."

"You'll do no such thing."

I don't think anybody had spoken a word, not among us prisoners, I mean, until Pa said that. He looked up from where he was sitting in the corner, his eyes blazing with hatred. "You'll not soil that flag with your grimy fingers. Not a man among you."

Laughing, Cassady flicked his toothpick at Pa's boots. "You'd try and stop us."

"You'll have to kill me before I let you soil that flag, you filth. And you sure won't burn it. Not while I'm alive."

The laugh died in Cassady's throat. He could see Pa meant it. Wasn't brag. My throat went dry as the dirt outside.

"It's a piece of cloth," Cassady said.

"To you. Not to me." Pa's head turned, and he looked straight at Julian, looked at him till Julian bowed his head. Pa started talking, not loud, not angry, just talking like he was telling a story, which he hardly ever did. Well, not this kind of story, I guess. Everyone listened, even those outlaws, and especially me. I hope I don't ruin his words. This is how he told it, best as I can remember.

"It was a beautiful morning. Not cold at all, not for February, but this was Mexico. Not a cloud in the sky, the sun just blazing. I remember that, see it clear as if it were yesterday. I can hear the bands playing 'Yankee Doodle' and 'Hail Columbia', and see old General Zachary Taylor riding Old Whitey, strutting like a peacock.

"Must have been an hour or so before noon when the Mexicans sent in this surgeon, and he started reading . . . I disremember his name . . . saying how we were surrounded by 20,000 men. The doc was a German, part Dutchy anyway. I think his mother must have been a Mexican. That Army captain you murdered last night reminded me of him, his accent and all, the way he carried himself. Old Santa Anna, the surgeon said, wanted 'to save you from catastrophe' . . . yes, sir, I recall those words. Those were the last words the doc got out before Old Zach cut him off, and I won't forget what he said.

" 'Tell Santa Anna to go to hell! Major Bliss' . . . Bliss was the adjutant, you see, William Bliss, good man . . . 'put that in Spanish for this damned Dutchman to deliver.'

"Well, that ended the talks, and three hours later, we were in full battle. Fought all day. Savage. Those Mexicans had us outnumbered, outgunned, but we fought like devils. Only darkness stopped the butchery. I remember being so tired. My face black as midnight from powder. So tired, but I couldn't sleep. Didn't even want to close my eyes. All night long, I could hear Santa Anna's soldiers crying out . . . 'Viva Santa Anna' . . . those poor, misguided fools. 'Libertad o muerte.' And hear something else, too, in Spanish and English. Men, men I'd rode with, men I'd been shooting at. Hearing their cries. Begging for water. For their mothers, *madres.* For death. Not long after that, Jeff Davis came, told us the general wanted to ride out and take a look-see at our defensive positions at Saltillo, make sure Santa Anna couldn't breach those, cut us off, strike us from behind. After that ride, I reckon I could have slept, just went to sleep forever, but then the Mexicans opened up with their eight-pounders. All night long. Come daylight, there was nothing beautiful about that dawn.

"They charged. The lines looked like they stretched all the way to the far end of Mexico, bayonets glistening in the sun, banners unfurling, lancers on horseback ready to strike, uniforms spotless, as if they'd just come into battle. Brave boys, those soldiers Santa Anna had. Never saw men die so brave. Those Mexicans. Our boys . . . from Illinois, Kentucky, Arkansas, and my fellow Mississippians. Must have been 1,000s, and those Mexicans came like a bolt of lightning.

"The Arkansans broke. Couldn't blame them at all. They dropped their muskets, mounted their horses, ran. Ran for Buena Vista, but Santa Anna was ready for that, and on came the lancers. Slaughter. No other word for that. Lancers cut most of them down. I reckon the whole Army would have been destroyed, wiped out, cut to pieces. Probably would have ended there if it hadn't been for those boys with the Illinois infantry. They didn't run. No, sir. They stood their ground and just gave those Mexicans buck and ball. Put a big hurt on Santa Anna's boys, but I reckon Santa Anna would have still won the day, but here came Old Zach.

"They called him Old Rough and Ready . . . that he was. Virginia-born, if I remember right, but Kentucky-raised, or maybe it was Tennessee. Grew cotton. Owned a plantation in Mississippi, had another home in Baton Rouge, but he was Army. He was a fighter. Why, I reckon he had seen more fighting than any man alive at Buena Vista. He'd fought in the War of 1812, the Black Hawk War, led the Army against the Seminoles down in Florida. I voted for him for President, you know. Guess he would have been a mighty good one, had he lived longer. Didn't look like a general, not Old Zach. Wore a straw hat with a wide brim and clothes that hadn't seen brush, water, or soap in months." Pa gave out a short chuckle. "Looked like the rest of us, I guess. Warrant that's why we all admired him so.

"Well, like I was saying, the general rides back about this time, and this officer, don't know who he was, came loping up beside him, reined in, his face filled with fear. 'General Taylor,' he says, 'we are whipped!' And Old Zach, he answers . . . 'I know it, but the volunteers don't know it. Let them alone. We'll see what they do.'

"Just then I saw this man. Oh, he wasn't a man, just a boy from Arkansas, carrying the colors, that flag you think you're game enough to burn, and I watched them Mexicans cut him down. There was nothing anyone could do, cut off from the rest of us like he was, but seeing that, hearing him cry for help, but always waving that flag, wondering, if he had thrown the flag aside, if he might could have gotten free. Probably not. It didn't matter. Reckon I just went clear out of my head, spurred my horse, and charged. Crazy. I heard Jeff Davis yelling for me to come back, others screaming that I'd be killed, but I didn't listen. Didn't care. One of those eight-pounders hit right about the time I reached those Mexicans. Killed the Mexicans. Killed my horse. Should have killed me, but it didn't. God was with me. My ears were ringing. I stood up, dazed, and the first thing I saw was the flag, lying on the ground, staff busted. I grabbed for it, took it off the busted pole, tied it to my rifle, and staggered back. I don't know how far it was, 200 yards maybe. Waving it over my head. Daring those Mexicans to come charging me, try to kill me. Jeff Davis and my Mississippi pards were no longer yelling at me. They were cheering, yelling hurrahs and huzzahs, cussing Santa Anna.

" 'You're wounded, Munro!' Jeff Davis says, and that I was. But I wasn't about to leave my friends, and I wasn't about to hand that flag to somebody else. Jeff and Old Zach saw that in my face, and they never pressed me on the subject.

"So Jeff Davis give us the command. And off we went.

"Proud, we were. In red shirts and white paints, armed with Bowie knives and our prized Mississippi rifles. We cut down those poor Mexican infantrymen. Battle they called it. More like murder. Then it looked to be us getting murdered. Lancers came right at us, lowering those spears, but I could hear Old Zach giving us the command . . . 'Steady, boys! Steady for the honor of old Mississippi.'

"Jeff Davis had us close the ranks, and we waited. Waited, watching those lancers come galloping toward us, waited until they were 80 yards from us, and then they did the strangest thing. They stopped. Just reined their horses to a stop. Jeff Davis, he later said that he suspected that it had been a trick, that the lancers were trying to draw our fire, that they didn't know the range of our rifles, figured we couldn't hit them at 80 yards, but they were wrong. Boy howdy, were they wrong. 'Fire!' Jeff Davis yells, and we fired. And that was murder. We killed them by the scores, killed them with one volley, men and horses, and then we watched them run.

" 'Well done!' the general was yelling, waving his hat. "Hurrah for old Mississippi!'

"And Jeff Davis rides over to me, and he shakes my hand, and I start to hand him the flag, present it to him, him being our commander and me slowing, getting some sense back in my head, but he says . . . 'No, Conner Munro. You earned that flag. It's yours, Mr.'

"There was more fighting to be done, and I did my share, till I'd lost so much blood they carried me, me and that flag, to the surgeon. It rained that afternoon, blessed rain, and the Battle of Buena Vista was over. They say we killed or wounded 3,500 Mexicans there. We had less than 300 dead, maybe 400 wounded.

"Well, I've carried that flag with me for 14 years, and I've carried something else with me. What I remember is Mississippians, Arkansans, Kentuckians, Illinoisans . . . all of us fighting together. We were Americans. Not Northerners. Not Southerners. Americans. Fighting together."

He nodded, satisfied, finished.

"That was another time," J.T. Cassady said, and he didn't say this mean or anything like that. I even thought he spoke with some measure of respect. "And this is another war."

Pa gave him a slight nod. "That may be, but you ain't touching that flag."

You couldn't hear anything for a minute or two, just the wind, and that flag popping outside.

"He's right, Cassady," Julian said at last from his seat. "We don't want to do anything that'll make the jehu on the stage tomorrow night suspicious. Marco Max will be expecting to see that flag."

"In the dark?"

"Moon will be up," my brother said.

"It ain't worth it, J.T.," Pinto told Cassady. He pointed the barrel of his revolver at Pa. "Look at that old bull. You'd have to kill him. And we might have need of him before this deal is done."

Cassady chewed on his lip, trying to stare down Pa, but he couldn't do that, so he gave a little shrug, and walked outside without another word. The flag had won. Pa had won.

I can hear the flag right now. Pa hasn't said anything since Cassady left. He's a prideful man, and, right now, I'm proud of him. Prouder than I've ever been.

February 27, 1861

This is the day. Time's running out. We have to figure out a way to stop them from robbing the stage. Stop Julian. But how?

At breakfast this morning, which was crackers and coffee, J.T. Cassady talked like he was a general, that this was the first strike for the Confederacy.

"After our victory, Arizona Territory will be open to all Southerners. This southern strip will give the Confederacy an avenue from Texas, all the way to California, with her vast riches and a port in the Pacific Ocean. I can then see a Confederate army striking northward from here, into New Mexico, all the way to the gold fields in Colorado."

I think Pa's right. These aren't soldiers. They're bandits.

The moon had gone full two days ago, and, with no clouds, it will be light out from the time the moon rose till it set, so those outlaws will have a good view from wherever they set up. Come 8:30, when the Westbound's due, it won't be dark at all.

Cassady pulled a big old watch from his pocket and checked the time, smiling, and I realized that it was Pa's watch, the solid gold watch he had bought when he had first taken the job with Mr. Butterfield, and I got hopping mad.

"You stole that!" I leaped to my feet. "That's my pa's watch, you low-down thief." I went straight for him, but Julian grabbed my arms and pinned them behind my back. Oh, I fought as hard as I could, trying to kick Julian's shins, fought even harder when J.T. Cassady, that miserable thief, laughed at me.

"It's all right, Smith," Pa said quietly, but it wasn't all right at all. Not to me.

"We're robbing the Army," Julian said firmly, still holding me, but looking straight at J.T. Cassady. "Not civilians. That's what you told me when you first approached me about this. Remember?"

They looked at each other long and hard, and I stopped kicking at my brother when J.T. Cassady pulled out the watch again and held it in his open palm. Julian let me go, and I walked over to Cassady, expecting him to drop the watch on the floor and crush it with the heel of his boot, but he didn't. He let me take it out of his hand, and I hurried back to Pa and handed the watch to him.

"Thanks, Son," he said, sliding the watch into his pocket.

Cassady laughed. "Twelve hours. Then the war begins."

Pa chuckled. "Maybe. What happens if the stagecoach can't get through?"

There hadn't been much conversation since those

vermin took us prisoner, but Pa was in the mood to talk, and I listened, wondering what he was trying to do. Me? I had no interest in conversing with pigs.

"I've watched the Overland in Tucson, sir," Cassady said. "And here. You can keep time by the stage-coaches almost as well as you can with your fancy watch."

"Sometimes. Not always." He pointed at the newspaper. "Take a gander at the *Times* . . . if you can read."

Cassady's face flushed, and he just stared at Pa, while Julian picked up the Mesilla paper.

"The Río Grande's rising," Pa said. "Next page. Rising rapidly."

Julian must have found the item, because he nodded. "I see that."

"If the jehu can't ford the river at the crossing, he's stuck at Fort Fillmore till the river goes down."

"You think I don't know about the ferry?" Cassady said.

"If the ferry's operating," Pa said. "But if the river's rising as high as it probably is from the snow melt and the rains up north, I'm not sure they'd be able to get a Celerity on the ferry. At least, I doubt if it will be here on time. They can make up time once they get to Yucca Flats. But the Overland Mail Company knows to be safe. We don't like our passengers drowning." He gave Howell a stern look. "Or getting shot."

"Reckon we'll just have to wait and see." Cassady tried to sound confident.

"Uh-huh. But then there's that other wagon. The payroll wagon, or what is supposed to be carrying the payroll. The wagon full of soldiers. It must be heading for Fort Tejon now, too." He pointed out the door. "Those Army boys travel the same road as the Overland. Likely to stop here for water. The dragoons have been camping here long before the Overland started running. The six of you plan on fighting off a squadron or two of dragoons?"

"If we have to, Munro. We are soldiers of the South."

Cassady walked outside, but he didn't strut so much.

Same day, noon

Well, I did it. Tried to escape. But they caught me.

It came to me, the idea, a little while after Cassady went outside. I figured Pa had been lying, trying to play with their nerves, figured that nothing, certainly not some high water between Fort Fillmore and La Mesilla, could stop good Overland men from getting a stage to a timetable stop on the Overland on time, or close to it. The more I thought on it, the more it struck me that somebody had to get out of here, get to the nearest station, warn them about what was happening here at Soldier's Farewell.

Pinto and J.T. Cassady were somewhere outside, and I figured Breed remained stationed up on the hill. Julian had gone somewhere, too. I think to talk to Pinto and Cassady, so that left us being guarded by Ben Jakes and the man with the eye patch, Howell. So without telling anyone what I aimed to do, I just stood up and walked over to the door. I could feel Pa's eyes staring at my back, could feel the rest of us prisoners watching me, wondering, worrying, and then Ben Jakes turned around and aimed that big pistol at my belly.

"What you think you're doin', boy?"

Howell put his hand on the hilt of his big Bowie knife, but he didn't say a thing.

"I have to go to the privy." I hoped my voice wouldn't quake with fear, but it did, and maybe that was for the better, make them think I was scared. Well, I was scared.

"Hold it," Ben Jakes snapped.

"I can't. I got to go," I said, almost whining. "Real bad."

That worthless Ben Jakes lowered the revolver he had stolen from Sergeant Scott and cackled. "Go in your pants," he said.

Well, a tear rolled down my cheek, and I quickly brushed it away, and I feared my plan wouldn't work at all, but then the Texican with the eye patch came to my defense. "Let him go," he said. I guess he thought I was nigh crying because of my bowels. Maybe he didn't want me to stink up the house.

Frowning, Ben Jakes shoved his pistol in his waistband and turned to Howell. "I ain't wet-nursin' this kid. Thinks he's better than me or anyone else. You take him!"

That would kill my plan right away. I didn't stand a chance of getting away with Howell guarding me, wasn't even sure I would have enough gumption to try it, remembering how he had shot down the man from Dallas.

Well, that big Bowie came out if its sheath in an instant, and Howell had the massive blade pressed against Ben Jakes's throat, had Jakes pushed against the door frame, and it was Ben Jakes, the sorry cur, who wound up wetting his britches.

"You don't give orders," Howell told him. "You don't never tell me what to do."

"What's going on here?" J.T. Cassady had walked up with Julian.

"It's a private matter," Howell said tightly, pressing the knife's point deeper into Ben Jakes's throat until a trickle of blood ran into the braggart's banded collar.

"Howell," Cassady said, "put that pig-sticker away. You almost ruined our plan when you killed that man down the road at the next station. Think, Howell, for once, just think! You would have had half the territory chasing you for murder if Munro here hadn't tracked you down, let everyone think the Apaches had killed you. We might have need of Mr. Jakes."

The knife vanished, and Howell turned away and glared at Cassady. He wasn't the type of man who liked to be told to do something by anyone, even his boss. He started to say something, choked it back, and tilted his head sharply at me.

"Boy here needs to do his business in the outhouse."

Cassady peered inside. "Take him," Cassady ordered Ben Jakes. "And clean yourself up, too."

I let out a big sigh, hadn't realized I'd been holding my breath all this time, filled my lungs with air, and passed Cassady through the door. I heard him tell Pa . . . "Were the soldiers at Buena Vista as insubordinate, as beetle-headed, as what I have under my command?"

The privy lies behind the big stone stables, just off the northwest corner. It's a two-seater, but I hoped Ben Jakes wouldn't come in with me, and he didn't, just held the door open for me and told me to hurry up, that he hadn't all day. Then he fingered the little nick in his neck, and held it there, looking like Howell had sliced his jugular.

Now, I hadn't really planned on what I'd do if I got this far. Wouldn't have time to grab Ivanhoe, or any mule, the gate being on the opposite end, and I had no idea where Pinto was all this time. Breed, from up on the hill, would have a good aim at me, but I wasn't certain he'd be able to hit me at that distance, although he would see me, could direct the rest to where I was. But just beyond the big wall of the stable ran the draw, and Breed couldn't see me through all the rocks and brush. I could hurry past the spring, just keep footing it, follow the draw, north maybe, follow it as far as I could, then cut out, dash behind Soldier's Farewell Hill. They wouldn't think of me doing that, I hoped. Make a beeline across the desert, keeping low, using yucca for cover, run those three miles across the open ground till I hit Burro Cienaga. Run for my life to Ojo de la Vaca. Get help.

I used the bathroom, surprised I had to after all that, buttoned my trousers, and just charged out the door. Ben Jakes cried out when the wooden door smashed his head, started cursing, and I started running.

"You lousy little . . . !" I couldn't hear the rest of Ben Jakes's words because the pistol shot drowned them out. Man, was I scared then, didn't think Ben Jakes would recover in time to shoot at me, but he did. The first shot went way wide, but the second one buzzed past my ear and whined off the rock wall. That got the mules on the other side of those rocks braying and squealing. Pa's prize stallion took off running and neighing, and one of his brood mares almost kicked down the wall in her stall. Sounded like that anyway.

The high stone wall ran forty feet. Forty feet to the draw. Felt like forty miles.

I heard others shouting then, but I just crashed through the brush, dropped into the draw, and ran. Another bullet smashed off a rock a few rods behind me. I knew this part of the station, it being right near the spring. Knew it well from all the time I'd spent out this way building the dam, then fixing it, fetching water. Another shot, then Cassady cursed Ben Jakes for being a fool. "Don't waste lead!" he yelled.

Somebody fired again, but this sounded farther off, from the station, maybe. I couldn't tell for sure.

I ran.

All of them couldn't come after me. They had to keep watch on Pa and the soldiers, Fletcher and Bartolomé. I figured Ben Jakes and Cassady were chasing me, but that might be enough. I had a good jump on Ben Jakes, who couldn't run fast after the pounding he had gotten, and, like I said, I knew this country better than they did.

I ran.

Three or four times, I stumbled. Rocks and cactus cut through my pants, left my knees bloody, but I didn't stay down long. I'd jump up, keep footing it, winding along the draw, my brogans pushing hard into the sand. Sweating. My throat parched. Knowing my feet would be bad blistered before long.

I ran.

Along about then, it struck me how they'd probably expect me to go this way, east I mean. Ojo de la Vaca was the closest station to us, five miles nearer than Barney's, and the stage that they planned on robbing would be coming from the east, so it made sense for me to light out that way. At that instant, I decided to change course, cut out the other way, run west. I knew a lot of those boys who worked at Barney's Station, knew how much Pa respected Mr. Barney.

It was nineteen miles to Barney's Station, nineteen open miles once I left the draw, nineteen miles of cactus, rocks, and, maybe, Apaches.

Nineteen miles. Criminy, I don't think I made it a mile.

The ringing of metal hoofs on the rocks sang out behind me, thundering, and I screamed like a little girl, knowing somebody horseback came after me, knowing I could never outrun horse or mule. I saw this grove of yucca, weaved in and out of it, hoping that would slow down my pursuer, and I reckon it did, but then I was back out in the open, running down a little hill, hearing the pounding hoofs draw closer, could hear the horse snorting, the rider cursing, and then felt the horse and rider right beside me, and I yelled out again, expecting a bullet in my spine, tried to duck, but a hand gripped my shirt, lifted me up, and I was tossed, smashed into the rocks, and figured I was dead.

When I came to, I saw Julian, his face drenched with sweat, felt him pressing a silk bandanna against my throbbing head, blood gushing from my forehead.

"You want to get killed?" Julian cried out at me.

Julian! He had ridden me down, not Howell or Breed, not any of those ruffians, but someone worse than them. My own brother.

I pushed the bandanna away, pushed him away, and shot to my feet, then fell right back down, the whole world spinning, blood pouring into my eyes.

"That was a fool thing to do!"

I didn't know what he meant. Standing up just

then? Well, yeah, it probably had been stupid. Running away? Maybe I would have made it had my treacherous brother not outsmarted me. He'd almost killed me himself.

"Come on!" He jerked me up, threw me onto the horse—Pa's fastest stallion, a big blood bay—and swung up in the saddle behind me.

"All you have to do is wait, Smith," he told me as we rode back to the station, me lying like a sack in front of him, his left hand pressing me down, blood dripping into my hair, onto the ground for the ants. "Wait a few more hours and this will all be over. I won't let them hurt you, but don't try anything like that again."

I laughed a little. "You didn't want that German captain killed, either," I told him. "That didn't stop them."

He pushed me down harder.

"Nice friends you got, Jules."

"Shut up! I'll fix your head when we get back to the station."

"You ain't touching me."

"Ain't is not a word. Remember?"

"Shut up. Some teacher you are. That captain was right. You are a traitor. To the Army. To your country. To me. To Pa. I hate your guts."

By then we'd reached the station, and Julian reined in, pulled me up roughly, then dumped me onto the dirt, pitched the bloody bandanna beside me, spurred the stallion, and loped off for the stable.

It was Pinto who helped me up, his hands gentle, and he brushed the dirt off the bandanna, and pressed it against my head, lifted my right hand, knuckles skinned, bruised, palm bleeding, and let me hold the rag against the wicked cut.

"You're game, kid," Pinto said. "I like that, respect that. But try that again and you'll wind up dead."

Walking inside, knowing I had failed Pa and the others, I wished I were dead.

Same day, half past 3 o'clock

Bleeding has stopped, but my head keeps pounding.

After Julian hauled me back to the station and Pinto helped me inside, I learned how I hadn't been the only body thinking of escape. Pa, Bartolomé, and the lieutenant were all hunched over the body of Sergeant Stone, and Mr. Fletcher lay, spread-eagle, a short distance away. Gasping, I wondered if I had gotten those two good men killed, but then I noticed Fletcher's chest rising and falling, and spotted a big knot forming on the side of his head.

"Smith!" Pa jumped up and ran, and Pinto backed up a couple of steps and put his hand on his revolver, but Pa didn't notice, and he wasn't going after no one, just me. He pulled me close, grabbed the bandanna, started working on the cut on my head.

"I'm all right," I said.

"Who did this?" Pa demanded.

As I write this, it strikes me funny. Reckon it struck me something similar then. Must have. I didn't answer at first, just watched Pa snatch a rag from his trousers pocket, and use it to wrap around my noggin, his hands gentle, trying not to hurt me, wiping the blood out of my eyes with Julian's silk rag.

"Who did it?" he asked again.

"I fell," I said. "The half-breed was chasing me." I just left Julian out of it. Did Pa know I was lying? I can't tell. He finished tightening the bandage, then leaned back, put both hands on my shoulders and gave a little nod as he examined me. I thought he was grading his doctoring skills, but that wasn't it at all.

"I'm proud of you," he said. "Though I don't want you to try anything like that again. Ever. Promise me!"

My head bobbed just slightly, though I reckon I was lying to my father again.

I asked him: "What happened here?"

Sergeant Stone groaned. At least he was alive, too.

Pa shot a glance at the sergeant, then over at Fletcher, who had lifted his left hand gently, moaning softly, and gently felt that growing lump, the skin tight and purplish.

The sergeant let out an oath, prompting a chuckle from Lieutenant Day, who said: "He'll be fine."

"Let's see to Mr. Fletcher," Pa said, and steered me to our hired man.

"How you feel?" Pa asked.

Fletcher blinked twice, and slowly shook his head. "Well. . . ." Sounded like he was considering some options.

"Pour some water on this." Pa handed me Julian's bandanna, and I went to the bucket, wet the rag, then brought it back to Pa, who started gently bathing Fletcher's wound.

"When we heard the shooting, the shouts," Pa said, "the sergeant and Fletcher here jumped up, made a rush for the door. Like they were expecting you to try something." Pa gave me a curious look. "I hadn't figured on it. Bartolomé and me, we tried to help out, but it was over in a heartbeat. That big man with the eye patch. . . ." Shaking his head, Pa pulled the wet cloth away from Mr. Fletcher.

"That hurt?"

"The barrel hurt a whole lot more," Fletcher said.

Pa placed the rag on the big bruised lump again. "Hold it here, Fletcher." He did as he was told. "You want some water? To drink?"

"No, sir. I'll be fine."

"Think you can sit up?"

"If it's all the same to you, sir, I'll just lie here for a spell. How's the Army fellow?"

Pa looked over at Sergeant Stone, Lieutenant Day, and Bartolomé. I did the same. They had pulled off the sergeant's tunic, ripped open his shirt, and were patching up a little hole in his left shoulder. I reckon the lieutenant had dug out the bullet, because Sergeant Stone was fingering it in his right hand.

"Looks like he'll live," Pa said.

Fletcher nodded ever so slightly.

"The big man." Pa returned to his story. "Howell, that's his name. He's a fast one. Thought we could jump him, his attention at the privy, but he heard us coming, shot the sergeant, then laid out Fletcher, here, with the barrel of his revolver. Bartolomé instinctively caught Stone as he was falling, and I, like a fool, just tripped over Fletcher when he dropped at my feet." Pa rubbed his own forehead, and I saw the scratch where he had skinned himself.

"Sorry about that," Fletcher said.

"Wasn't your fault."

"Well," Fletcher said, "reckon that Texican could have shot us all down."

Pa's head shook thoughtfully. "No," he said in a whisper. "They need us alive. That's why he didn't kill us. Need us for when the stage arrives."

A short while later, Cassady walked in, surveyed the scene, and clucked his tongue. "I trust, gentlemen, that we'll have no more displays of stupidity."

Nobody answered him. Other than me, no one even looked at him, and he shook his head, turned quickly, and marched outside, barking orders to Ben Jakes, Pinto, and Howell.

"All that scratchin' makes me nervous," Howell just told me.

"You best give that pencil a rest."

I kept right on writing.

"Boy! Stop writin'. . . ."

"Leave him alone." Julian keeps pretending he's my defender.

They're back inside, most of them. Haven't seen the half-breed, still atop the hill, I reckon, and Ben Jakes is outside. I can hear him whistling and shuffling his boots.

"What's he writin'?"

Julian tossed the dregs of his coffee in the spittoon. "His innermost thoughts. His hopes and dreams. Leave him be."

Howell spit on the floor. "If he writes down our names and descriptions, the law can. . . ."

"Union law," Julian said. "It won't hold in the Confederate States of America. Once we're in Texas, we're free. So let him write."

With a grunt, Howell turned and left, and I could feel Julian staring at me, wanting me to know how he had protected me, wanted me to write all I wanted to write. So I'm putting down this pencil, and shutting the journal, and I'm going to just stare at him, and let him know what I think of him, my wicked big brother.

Same day, 6 o'clock

Somehow, I had fallen asleep, but a shot rang out, and I jumped, wide awake.

Had it been a dream? No, because a tenseness filled the station. We prisoners were back against the wall, looking, wondering, but Ben Jakes and Howell, guarding the doorway, started talking, pointing, and I heard Cassady yell out: "Where did that come from?"

No one could answer him.

Cassady cursed. A mule brayed. The leader of those ruffians cursed again, louder, nervous. "Someone's comin'!" I think Pinto must have shouted that. Cassady barked at Howell and that no-good Ben Jakes to get inside, and they did.

From inside the doorway, Ben Jakes pointed, and Howell grunted.

"By jingo, what if it's that wagon full of dragoons?" Ben Jakes kept shaking, sweating, his Adam's apple bobbing as he tried to swallow down his fear. "What if . . . ?"

"It ain't the Army, you yellow. . . ." Howell choked back his curse. "Just a speck of dust. One rider."

But who?

I wet my lips, longing to know that answer, wanting to get up, see the dust for myself, but knew I couldn't.

"Watch 'em!" Keeping his eyes trained outside, Howell motioned toward us, and Ben Jakes, trying to look brave, kept that stolen pistol in both hands, staring at us, but never for long. Always, he'd look back at Howell, try to see over the big man's shoulder, find out who was coming.

I wondered if we should try to rush them again.

No, not with Howell quick as a cat. Wounded as they were, Mr. Fletcher and Sergeant Stone wouldn't be of much help. All we could do was sit and wait. And worry.

Lifting his revolver, thumbing back the hammer, Howell stepped back slightly.

Slow hoof beats sounded, and Ben Jakes squeaked out, "What . . . who?"

"Quiet!" Howell said in a harsh whisper. A moment later, he snorted, lowered the hammer, and stepped outside. "It's Breed," he announced.

Ben Jakes let out a little giggle of relief, and quickly found a chair, waving the pistol in our direction and warning us not to make any sudden moves. I thought about asking him if he had wet his britches again, but decided against provoking him. Besides, the men outside had started talking to Breed.

"What happened?" Pinto asked, but then someone said: "Who's the *hombre?*"

I looked at Pa, but he didn't say anything, just tried harder to listen.

"Breed," Cassady began. "I told you . . . who is it? What happened?"

"He's a quiet *hombre.* I respect this *hombre.*"

"You shoot him?"

"Who else?"

Well, after that, Cassady and Breed continued talking, but too muffled for me to make out much of anything.

Right then, it struck me, and I knew who they were talking about, knew it with my heart, dreading it, and when they dragged in the dark-skinned man, Pa swore and Bartolomé practically cried.

"You should have stayed with the horses, Nicanor," Cassady snapped at the half-breed. "You put us all at risk."

Breed shrugged, and grinned.

Pa and I were up, running to *Señor* Vee, rolling him over, terrified at the ghastly hole in his side. Lieutenant Day and Bartolomé came over, and we lifted Tori's dad, brought him to the corner. Fletcher was up, weak as he was, but he fetched the bucket of water.

"He came sneaking up," Cassady said. "Suspicious. Nicanor says he was pretty good." The Southron laughed slightly. "Just not as good as my man here." He patted the half-breed on the back, the same man he had just criticized for not staying at the Velásquez place with the horses.

Pa had pulled up the blood-soaked homespun shirt. He looked at Cassady. "We need whiskey. Clean the wound."

"Why? In an hour he'll be with his ancestors."

Ignoring Breed, Pa looked hard at Cassady. "Whiskey!" he demanded, but those men just sauntered out the door, with Cassady calling back with a laugh: "We ain't wastin' good whiskey on a Mexican, Munro!"

Now, I stare at my hands, stained with blood. My own blood, and *Señor* Vee's. He's in the corner, sleeping, covered with blankets. We've done all we can for him. It's hard to think about it all.

When Cassady and the others left, leaving Ben Jakes and Pinto to guard us, Pa told me to put on some water to boil, then he hurried to the kitchen and pulled out a knife.

"You best put that down." Ben Jakes thumbed back the hammer of his revolver.

Pa ignored him. He stuck the blade in the coals.

"Put it down!"

"He ain't gonna stick you, Jakes," Pinto said lazily. "Let them work on the greaser. He's a good man, I warrant. Better than you."

That's what we did. About 10 minutes later, Julian walked in. The bullet had gone clear through *Señor* Vee, and we had cleaned it up as best we could. Julian knelt over the unconscious man, the man I'd always figured would wind up being his father-in-law, and he was shaking, Julian was, tears welling in his eyes.

"I didn't. . . ." He shook his head, reached inside his hunting shirt, and pulled out a flask. "Here."

Pa snatched it from him without looking, without thanking him. He unscrewed the cap and poured the whiskey into the bullet hole.

Unconscious, Alyvia's daddy screamed, then dropped into a deeper sleep.

"Fetch the knife," Pa told me.

Julian had backed away, unable to watch, and he was gone by the time I brought the knife back. The others knew what was coming, because they took hold of *Señor* Vee's arms and legs, holding him down. The knife blade looked hotter than the desert wind in August. "Lay the flat side over the hole," Pa told me. "Quickly."

Can't get the smell out of my nostrils. Can't forget the noise. The muted groans of agony. The terror. I burned that bullet hole, like, well, like nothing I know. Then, like a silly girl, I just sank down on the floor. My eyes rolled back in my head, and I was out like *Señor* Vee.

I woke to Bartolomé pressing a wet rag on my cheeks. Those cheeks turned red quickly when I realized what I had done. Passed out. Just plumb sat down and fainted. Pa, or somebody, had heated the blade again and sealed the exit wound in *Señor* Vee's back. Cauterized it, Lieutenant Day said. I reckon they hadn't had to burn Sergeant Stone's shoulder like that. He hadn't been bleeding as badly as *Señor* Vee, though.

"How . . . will he . . . is he going to . . . ?" I couldn't talk straight, couldn't summon up the words.

Pa was beside me again. "You all right?"

"Yes, sir. I'm sorry I. . . ."

"I shouldn't have had you do it. That was my fault." He pressed his hand on my shoulder and squeezed it. "You did fine, Smith."

Same evening, must be right around 8:30

Well, it's full dark now. Moon's rising. A short while ago, Cassady came inside with the others and laid down his rules—what was expected of us, what was going to happen.

"When the stagecoach comes in, you'll act just like always. We've even done some of your work for you. The team's hitched and ready. Nicanor will be watchin' from somewhere close, and. . . ." Grinning, he nodded at the still-sleeping *Señor* Vee, and continued: "You all know what fine work that half-breed does. Moonlight'll give him a clear shot at anyone outside. Howell and Pinto will have y'all covered. Move and you're dead. Shout a warnin' and you're dead. Try anything. Julian will be with y'all, workin' just like always. Only Julian'll have a gun, and he's a mighty fine shot, too." He had walked over to me, and put his hand on my head, messing up my hair.

"Try one thing stupid, and I'll put a bullet in the boy's brain. Remember that.

"You usher the passengers inside, where Mr. Jakes and I'll be waitin'. We get the money from the soldiers, and we be on our way. Nobody gets hurt. We relieve the Union tyrants of some money, which we deliver to the Confederacy for honor and glory. You can spend the rest of your days enjoyin' this . . . paradise."

No one said anything. We waited.

Stage is coming. Just heard the shout. Don't know what'll happen. God willing, we'll stop them. Stop Julian. If not. . . .

March 24, 1861

Back home at Soldier's Farewell. I burned the *McGuffey's New Fourth Eclectic Reader* that Julian gave me, and came close to tossing this diary in the flames, as well, but. . . .

Been ages since I wrote in this. Plenty of news.

We carried *Señor* Vee, still unconscious, to my bunk, and left Sergeant Scott with him, along with Ben Jakes as their guard. Pa went out with the rest of them, even Fletcher, who remained groggy from the wallop Howell gave him earlier.

Inside, I waited, fear gnawing the insides of my stomach something terrible.

Outside, came the pounding of the hoofs, the jingling of traces, growing steadily, and soon I heard commotion and curses, just like always whenever a stage arrived. I sat alone in the station with Cassady, a Pocket Colt aimed in my direction though his attention remained outside as he listened, just as I did, nervous with anticipation, or just plain nervous.

Waiting for a shot, I braced myself. Not a shot at me, but somewhere outside. It never happened, though. The door swung open, and folks started filing inside, weary and grouchy like normal, unaware of what was happening, and Cassady backed himself into the corner, hiding his little revolver inside a coat pocket, warning me with his eyes not to say a word.

I'm not sure how I felt about all this. Disappointment? Anger? Hard to say. Deep down, I had hoped Pa and the others would try something, warn those soldiers carrying the payroll disguised as civilians, jump Pinto and Breed, disarm them. Something like that. On the other hand, I didn't want them to try anything because it would be fruitless. I didn't want Pa to get killed.

"Where's the grub and coffee?" a bald gent in a dust-covered broadcloth suit shouted. Another asked about the privy, and then Howell slipped inside, quietly drawing his pistol.

I said nothing. I counted 9 passengers, kind of a low number considering how many folks had been traveling on the Overland in recent weeks, seven men and two women, one of the latter silver-haired and dressed in black like she must have been a widow, the other middle-aged, hanging on the arm of a younger man with a thick brown mustache.

"The privy?" the gent in plaid britches and a striped shirt repeated, embarrassed.

"You'll have to wait." Howell thumbed back the hammer.

"What's the meaning of this?" exclaimed the bald man, indignant.

Cassady showed his pistol, aiming it at the three men he figured were the couriers, and he sure had that figured right.

"Shuck your hardware," Cassady said, his voice surprisingly high-pitched. Nerves, I reckon. "All of you. Do something quick, and you're dead. We've got 40 men outside!"

Ben Jakes showed himself, along with the revolver he had stolen, keeping the two wounded men in the corner of his eye, making himself look big and brave.

"Now!" Cassady stretched his arm, putting the barrel close to a passenger's face.

"I said . . . ," began the uppity gent, but he never got to finish.

"Shut up!" Howell barked. "One more word from you, Mr., and you'll never say another."

The silver-haired woman gasped, and I thought the man in need of the privy would wet himself.

Then Pa filed in, followed by Bartolomé, Lieutenant Day, Mr. Fletcher, Marco Max, and Little Terry, all holding their hands high, and they walked to the wall near me, and sat down, clasping their hands behind their heads, just as they had been instructed. Pinto and Breed followed them, guns out.

"Your weapons, gentlemen," Cassady instructed again. "Drop them at your feet, then kick them toward my associate." His head tilted toward Pinto.

At last, the sidearms fell to the floor, and Breed picked them up and stuck them in his waistband. Outside, a mule hee-hawed, then sounded like it just screamed. I wondered what Julian was doing all this time.

"Now, I'll relieve you three gentlemen of your money belts, while our associates are finding the money you've hidden in your grips on the stage-coach." Cassady watched, smiling, enjoying this moment, his voice dropping to its normal pitch. When the young fellow with the brown mustache, traveling with one of the ladies, started for his own belt, Cassady told him to stop.

"We don't rob civilians, sir." Cassady smiled with pride. "This is a strike for the Confederate States of America, the first battle in Arizona Territory, the first fight for liberty." I think he had practiced that statement.

The man who thought he was being robbed let out a sigh of relief, but then Howell spoke up. "Wait a minute, Capt'n." He walked over to the couple, addressing the man. "Where you from?"

The man wet his lips. The lady, clinging to his arm, squeezed tighter.

"Oh- . . . Ohio."

"Yankee!" Howell spit. "I reckon we'll take that belt, after all. And your fancy watch. And your sweetheart's broach."

Pursing his lips, Cassady started to object, but he didn't want to quarrel with Howell, ruthless as that big man could be.

"Vermin!" the older lady said.

Howell eyed her. "And where are you from, ma'am?"

"Trash!" She spit on his boots. "Swine. Filth!"

"I asked you where you was from." Howell showed no emotion as he tapped the pistol's barrel on a dainty watch dangling from the woman's neck on a silver chain. "You ain't Southern, that's certain sure. Right pretty," he said, resting the revolver's barrel on the face of the watch. "Reckon I'll take it."

"Leave her be." It was Pinto who spoke. "Take the man's money and watch if you want," he said when the one-eyed man turned toward him, glaring. "But leave the woman alone. And you're not taking the other lady's broach."

The two gunmen eyed each other, and I hoped they'd start shooting each other, but I guess Howell desired no quarrel with Pinto, so he picked up the money belt the man had dropped, snatched his gold watch, and left the two women alone, the younger one trembling, the older one defiant as blazes.

"That's right," Cassady said. "As Southern men, we are brought up to respect the fairer sex. My apologies, ladies. Mr. Howell sometimes forgets his place, his manners."

Yeah, I thought, eying Cassady with growing contempt. You didn't say one thing till Pinto spoke up. You're as big a coward as Ben Jakes.

Howell leaned against the wall, his face a chunk of granite.

All this time, the three couriers had reluctantly dropped their money belts, which Cassady and Ben Jakes now picked up. As Cassady hefted one, his grin widened. "Heavy," he said. "The boys at Fort Tejon will be sorely disappointed. Now, everyone, join the Overland hands at the wall. Hands locked behind your heads, and all of you sitting on the floor. Ladies, you may stand where you are, but please don't move, and I'm afraid I must also ask you to keep your hands held high. Munro!"

A moment later, Julian stuck his head in the door. "Horses and mules ready?"

"Yes, sir," my brother answered.

"The stage?"

"Crippled. They'll have to replace two wheels."

So that's what my treacherous brother had been doing.

"Good." He nodded at Pinto and Breed, who stepped outside and past my brother. When Julian started to go with them, Cassady told him to wait, but first he had to warn the rest of us. "We'll be taking our leave," he said. "The first battle of the war has been bloodless, and I'd like to leave here without having to kill anyone."

I held my tongue. Bloodless? What about the German captain they had murdered? What about Sergeant Scott and *Señor* Vee wounded? What about Fletcher getting buffaloed, and me getting my head busted open?

"We'll be outside," Cassady went on, "riding off to glory, but I'm leaving the half-breed behind with instructions to kill any man foolish enough to stick his head outside. He has Mr. Munro's Mississippi Rifle and plenty of other weapons. Two hours. That's all you have to wait. Then Nicanor will be gone to join us, and you can return to your travels."

He waited. No one spoke.

With a signal from Cassady, Ben Jakes and Howell walked outside, with Howell relieving Jakes of the two money belts he had draped over his shoulders.

"Munro!" Cassady called to my brother.

"Sir?"

I tried not to show any emotion as Cassady walked to me, knelt, and, keeping the revolver pointed at my head with his right hand, reached over with his left and snatched the diary, the pencil falling out by his feet. Quick, he was. I'll say that for him. I started to protest, realized the hopelessness of that, and determined not to give him any satisfaction. He was up, away from us, reading silently as he'd flip over a few pages, read some, flip over some more, stop and read again. Reading my thoughts. Reading stuff not meant for him. I hated that bandit. I cursed him silently, and I cursed Julian as the cause of all this.

Cassady managed fairly well, using that one hand, keeping the Pocket Colt trained on us, but not looking at us, just reading bits here and there. At last, he tossed the diary to my brother, who tried to catch it, but missed, and it fell on the floor. As Julian picked it up, Cassady looked at me. "Your writing skills have improved, my friend," he said. "At least your understanding of grammar. Some. You learn fast. And your descriptions of us might prove handy for the authorities. So we'll take this with us. Your brother will carry it with him. Give him something to read over the next few weeks until we whip the Yankees and preserve the rights of the South."

Tucking my diary underneath his arm, Julian said softly: "Like I've said, Federal law can't touch us in the South. Let Smith keep his diary."

Cassady clucked his tongue. "We're not in Texas yet."

"It's not far."

"Far enough. You can mail it back to him when we're in Austin. Or even Janos, perhaps."

"But. . . ."

"Can you follow an order, Munro?" Cassady barked with rage.

Looking down, Julian started to join the others outside.

"One more thing, soldier!" Cassady called to my brother. "After we ride out, go to the stable. Kill the mules."

I started to jump up, but Pa grabbed my shoulder, pulled me down. So I yelled: "You can't do it!"

They didn't listen to me.

"They can't take the stagecoach anywhere," Julian protested. "And Breed will give us time. . . ."

"They can ride the mules, Munro," Cassady fired back. "Ride to the next station, ride to Fort Fillmore for all I know, ride to the dragoons."

"But Breed. . . ."

"Kill the mules! All of them! This is war, mister, and it's a long ride to freedom, to victory. Kill them!" He was shouting those orders as he stormed outside, pushing Julian aside, disappearing. Silence.

Then Cassady's voice again: "Victory! Long live Jefferson Davis! Long live the South!"

More hoofs, followed by nothing but the wind, nothing but Julian staring at us, till Pa stared him down. My brother swallowed. "Remember Breed's outside," Julian warned. "Don't try anything."

The door closed.

Quickly the three couriers reached behind them, drawing pistols they had secreted in shoulder holsters, boots, or behind their backs.

"How'd they know?" one of the soldiers asked Lieutenant Richardson.

"They knew," he answered flatly, standing, joining his fellow soldiers.

"Traitors!" one of the soldiers said.

"Filth!" the old lady repeated.

"You civilians," the oldest soldier said, "I want you to go inside that room there. Stay low. Keep quiet." He looked at Pa. "Sir, do you have any weapons?"

Pa, still sitting, still holding me, shook his head slowly. "They took what we have after they captured us. Colt revolvers, couple of shotguns, revolving rifles, and my old Mississippi Rifle."

"They killed Captain Beckenbauer," Richardson Day said. "Murdered him. Didn't give him a chance. Wounded my sergeant." He pointed at Sergeant Scott, who had stepped into the main room.

"Shot another good man who lives nearby," added Fletcher, nodding toward my bunk.

One of the soldiers stood by the closed door. "You think he was bluffing?" he asked with hesitation. "About leaving a man behind?"

Sergeant Scott came up to the door. "I'll help," he said.

That's when the gunshots started from the stable.

I fell back, crying, because you could hear more than just shots, and Pa pulled me close, and I wanted to just stay there, crying, but it was like all I could hear were those screams. My brother stood in the stable, killing our mules, our breeding stock, Pa's love. Butchery!

"No!" I cried, and started for the door, pulling away from Pa's grasp, wanting to go outside, not caring about Breed, ignoring the warning, the threat. Someone stopped me. I thought it was Pa, but turned to see Bartolomé, saying something in Spanish, while Pa just sat there, listening, rigid, tears welling in his eyes.

"Let's go!" Lucas Scott jerked open the door. Ducking, the sergeant, unarmed, bolted outside, and the other soldier started to follow him, but a rifle spoke, and he dropped in the doorway. Musketry continued. A bullet spanged off the top of the doorway. Another splintered the leg of Pa's chair.

The younger lady screamed.

"Stay down!" someone yelled.

A rifle roared. Breed was well-armed.

Another soldier got to the door, firing into the night. Then the third man, the oldest soldier, crouched beside him, shooting. "Go after the sergeant!" He pulled the trigger, and the other one leaped out the door. I lost count of the shots. A bullet whined off the rock.

Mules screamed.

Bartolomé released his grip. Smoke burned my eyes, but that's not why I was crying. Another ricochet.

"Somebody!" the soldier said from the door as he fired, ducked, aimed again. "Get Benson out of here!"

Fletcher and Marco Max ran over, without caution, grabbed the downed soldier's arms, dragged him from the opening, rolled him over. Little Terry busied himself rifling through the room, looking for something to shoot with, but that was no use.

"He's dead!" Fletcher said.

The younger woman gasped, and Marco Max closed Benson's eyes, whipped off his own jacket, covered the dead man.

Mules screamed. I wonder if I really heard them, with all the gunfire, the shouts, ricochets, curses. Wonder if I heard those mules being shot down, or if it were only in my mind.

"What can I do?" Marco Max yelled.

The sound of slaughter continued, grew louder, deafening.

Another gun spoke, and I realized Lieutenant Day had picked up the dead soldier's revolver.

"What can I do?" Marco Max yelled again.

"Nothing!" the shooting soldier said. "Not unless you have a gun!"

I looked at Pa. He just sat there, tears streaming down his face.

Mules screamed.

And I ran outside.

The oldest soldier focused on reloading his pistol, and a shot from Breed had kicked dirt into Lieutenant Day's eyes. Those are the only reasons I made it out the door.

"Smith!" Pa screamed, but I was gone.

Immediately a gun barked, a bullet buzzed over my left shoulder, and I stumbled toward the side of the house, falling face down in the dirt. Another shot, but this one must not have been aimed at me. Suddenly, savagely rough hands grabbed my shirt, dragged me to the side of the house. A bullet whined off the rock wall.

I heard heavy breathing.

"You . . . fool . . . kid!"

I looked up at Sergeant Lucas Scott.

"Smith!" Yet another shot answered Pa's yell. My bravery, or tomfoolery, had broken whatever grip it was that had weakened Pa.

"He's all right!" Scott yelled. "I've got him."

More gunfire sang out somewhere in the darkness. The sergeant and I pressed as hard as we could against the wall, made as poor a target as we could for Breed, wherever he was hiding and shooting, but I kept contemplating my next move. The side door to the stables lay just a few yards away, the door closed, but I ought to chance it. I had to. That close to all of Pa's animals. I could make it. I knew I could. I just had to make it. To stop Julian. To save Pa's stock.

Sergeant Scott must have read my mind, because he pressed down hard on my shoulder and said:

"That door's barred shut, boy. I tried it. Like to have gotten killed."

"The front then!" I barked at him.

I'd go around to the gate, get inside that way.

"You'd never make it. That half-breed would cut you to pieces before you got to the wall. Or your brother inside. That breed came mighty close to killing me. And he. . . ."

"We could. . . ."

"Forget it. This fight's all but over. Those boys have won, for now. Thing we got to do is stay alive."

I couldn't hear the mules any more.

Hoofs sounded, and a horse and rider thundered out of the gate, heading away from the house. He must have turned around the corner and loped around the back of the stable, avoiding getting shot by the soldiers in the house. Riding around the back, he cut around the rear and galloped not 20 yards from us.

Julian!

Unarmed, the sergeant and I could only watch hopelessly as he disappeared. I don't know what Sergeant Scott thought he could do, running outside without a weapon. That had been as stupid as my bolt out of the house. Looking around for the other soldier who had followed the sergeant outside, I finally spotted him propped up against the right rear wheel of Marco Max's Celerity. At first I thought he was just hugging the stagecoach tight for cover, but then I knew. He was dead.

I saw something else, too—the team of mules, still in their traces, in front of the coach. Julian had done more than just busted up two wheels. He, or someone else, but one of his *compadres*, had killed every one of those mules, slitting their throats while they stood there in harness, worn out, trusting, helpless.

"Maybe the Apaches'll butcher ever' last one of them," Sergeant Scott said dryly as the hoof beats from Julian's mount faded away.

"Yeah," I heard myself telling Sergeant Scott. "I hope the Apaches kill them all."

For the next half hour, an eerie silence filled the night. No more shots were fired. I looked at the stable, its high stone walls looking haunted in that moonlight, with a sickening in my gut. Deeper than that, I think. I had wanted to run to the stable, stop my brother, end the slaughter, but I couldn't do anything.

We waited.

Maybe 10 more minutes passed, then Sergeant Scott said something to me that I didn't really hear, and he stood up, hesitant at first, braced his back against the wall, and peered around the corner. For what seemed an eternity he stood there, then his Adam's apple bobbed, his fingers tightened into fists, and he stepped out into the open.

Swallowing down fear, I told him to get down, that Breed would shoot him dead, reminded him that Cassady said the Breed would wait two hours, and not an hour had passed.

"He's gone," the sergeant said, but he didn't sound like he believed it much.

He walked to his dead companion by the wagon, swore softly, picked up the revolver, and stepped into the open. "They're all gone!" he shouted, and Lieutenant Day and Pa stepped outside, equally uncertain, followed by the other soldier. I shut my eyes tight, knowing with all my heart that Breed sat out there somewhere, waiting patiently for all the men in the station to step outside, lulling them into a false security, waiting to kill every last one of us, shoot us down in the open.

Pa knelt beside me. "You all right?" he asked.

Eyes shut tight, I could barely nod.

"Marco!" I heard Pa yelling. He was standing, moving with the others, taking command. "We got to get the wheels fixed. I got spares in the stable. You menfolk! We'll need your help. Ladies, get some coffee boiling. How's the soldier yonder?"

"Dead," Sergeant Scott said.

Pa muttered an oath.

When I forced my eyes open, I found myself looking into Pa's stern stare. He was back beside me, waiting, maybe thinking of something to say, but remaining quiet. In the moonlight, I could see the paths tears had traced down his dirty face, but he wasn't crying any more.

"Come on, Smith." He held out his hand. "There's work to do."

I let him lift me to my feet, then followed him, my heart sinking as we approached the stable gate.

"Buck up," he quietly told me. "We got to work through this. You and me, both. There's men to be buried. The coach to fix. Maybe. . . ."

We went inside.

I don't think I'll ever get free of that smell, ever forget the sight of those mules, donkeys, and horses. Gunsmoke, blood, and manure. The smell of death. The sight of savagery.

The outlaws had stolen our best stock, the stallions, the fastest horses and mules. On the wall of

the room that served as quarters for our crew, Pa
fetched a whale-oil lantern, turned up the flame,
told me to go inside and fetch a hammer and wrench,
which I did. When I came outside with the tools, Pa
stood where I had left him, holding the lantern up,
looking, not wanting to believe, not wanting to see.

He hoped—I guess we both had prayed—Julian
would have surprised us, done something decent
for once in his life, disobeyed Cassady's cruel order.
Yet all we saw at first were dead animals.

My heart sank at the thought of my brother's
mule, Sweet Ainsley, and I feared finding that beautiful Tobiano amid the carnage.

Above our heads, the ragged flag Pa had fetched
at Buena Vista popped in the cool wind, and I
thought of Pa telling us how a man could depend on
his sons, and I thought of how wrong he was.

Because of Julian.

Then I saw one of the dead animals, and I couldn't
help it, couldn't fight back the tears, and I dropped
to my knees, just bawling.

"He . . . Ju- . . . he . . . killed. . . ."

No, it wasn't Sweet Ainsley. It was a sorrel mule,
long ears, rather silly looking, a bit temperamental
who'd eat more than a jackstock man could really
afford.

"He killed . . . Ivanhoe!"

Pa sat beside me, pressed a hand on my shoulder.
He glanced at my mule—my mule!—head shot,
lying as if had wanted to roll in the dust. Pa took a
deep breath, slowly exhaled. "Yes, he did, Son. But
we have to press on. Smith, there's work to do." He
helped me up, and we continued.

We didn't find Sweet Ainsley. Now that I could
think back on it, I realized Julian had ridden off on

that great Tobiano. Two mules were still alive, but, shot up as they were, I knew Pa'd have to come back with a gun and put those poor beasts out of their misery. Some lay against the slab walls. Others sprawled in the center, but near the flagpole, we found three donkeys alive. Not even shot. Scared, but alive. Maybe Julian had run out of powder and lead. Maybe he'd run out of time. Or lacked the grit to finish the job. Maybe there had been some decency in him.

It didn't matter. Three jennies out of two dozen horses, mules, and donkeys. If that's decency. . . .

We got the jennies out of the stable, along with the spare wheels and some tools. Usually Pa would breed a male donkey with a mare, but sometimes he'd have one of his stallions couple with one of these jennies to breed what most mule men called a hinny. 'Course, it took longer to get a jenny in the family way, but Pa was patient about these kinds of things. The donkeys struggled, fighting over the smell of blood, but calmed down once we cleared the gate and hobbled them on the far side of the stable, away from the dead mules still hitched to the Westbound stage.

"We'll take those mules," the oldest soldier said. "I am Lieutenant James B. Trenton, sir. We'll go after those bandits."

Ignoring him, Pa told Marco Max: "How long to fix the wheels?"

"We'll get her done, Mr. Munro."

"The mules . . . ," Lieutenant Trenton said.

"They're donkeys, bub."

"Be that as it may, we need them now. It's our duty, and your duty to. . . ."

"I don't care what you need, Trenton." Pa stood

straighter, and the lieutenant backed away. Guess he thought Pa would be weak, but Pa's old self had returned. Certainly he wasn't the same man who had been so hurt and weak back in the station house.

"My duty's to the Overland Mail Company, a company that you, sir"—Pa jabbed a finger in Trenton's chest—"and the Army put at risk. We don't carry payrolls. Not on the Overland. You disregarded that." His hand swept out toward some of the passengers who had ventured outside. "You could have gotten these people killed. I have a schedule to keep, sir, and I'm keeping it as best as I can." He turned back to the jehu. "Marco, I'm giving you two mules. You'll have to nurse them to Barney's."

"Will do it."

"Tell him what happened here. Take these fool soldiers with you. Maybe Barney can spare some stock for them. Bartolomé!"

"*Sí, señor.*"

"You need to ride to Ojo de la Vaca. Ride fast. Tell them what happened here, that those butchers have stolen or killed most of our stock. We need a team here for when the Eastbound comes through. Need some firearms, too. And any men he can spare. *¿Comprende?*"

"*Sí, Señor* Conner."

"Good. Light out. Watch for Apaches. And those bandits might be headed that way, too, might have doubled back to the east. *Vaya con Dios.*"

The soldier started to protest again, thought better of it, and sighed in defeat. Pa glared at him. "Moon's still up," he said. "You want to bury your two men?"

"I guess."

"Fletcher, show him where the graveyard is. Couple of you soldier boys can dig the graves, the rest of y'all can drag these dead mules out yonder. You men!" he yelled at the gentlemen passengers. "Lend a hand." Then looked at me. "Smith, you and me'll help Marco and Little Terry." Back to the soldiers. "Get moving. Time's a-wasting. Quicker we get that coach fixed, quicker you get to Barney's and can go after those. . . ." He spit.

Before Pa could squat down to assist with the wheel, however, the older woman from the stagecoach stepped into the doorway. "Mr. Munro?" she called out tentatively.

"Yeah?"

"The Spanish gentleman. The one in the bed who has been dreadfully wounded. He's awake, sir, asking to speak to you."

It must have been midnight, probably later, by the time the two wheels were fixed, the two jennies hitched to the Celerity, and the passengers loaded.

"Can you make it with two donkeys?" Pa asked Marco Max as he climbed into the driver's box.

"I'll make it. Have to go easy. Make some of those gents walk a time or two."

"You know what's best."

"Good luck."

"Luck to you, Marco." Pa handed him a note. "Send that on to Giles Hawley in Tucson. We'll need mules to replace those Julian killed or stole."

The jehu shoved the letter into his pocket. "Will do."

Lieutenant Trenton helped the ladies into the coach, then looked at Pa. "Mr. Day says one of those bandits was your son."

"He was. Was a dragoon, too. That's how he knew your plans."

"Does he know this area?"

"Some. I warrant those other *hombres* know it better. I warrant Smith here knows this country better than Julian."

Maybe the lieutenant decided he couldn't trust Pa, though I don't know why, and he looked at me. "Do you know where your brother's going?"

I shot Pa a look, but his face remained a rock, and the lieutenant was telling me, ordering me, to answer him, not to look at my father.

"I. . . ."

"Son." Trenton decided to try sympathy. "I don't want to hurt your brother."

A bitter thought swept through my mind: I do!

"I don't think he meant for this to happen. Not all of it. But that money . . . well . . . where would you go?"

I fought the urge to look again at Pa, shuffled my feet, then said. "I . . . well. . . ."

Earlier, Lieutenant Day and Trenton had discussed the same subject. The robbers had ridden out west, but Day suggested they'd double-back, make a beeline for Texas and the Confederacy, but Trenton thought they might head to Tucson, it being full of Southern sympathizers and secessionists, and avoid pursuit from patrols out of Fort Fillmore. That didn't make much sense to me—there were forts out west, too—but Trenton remained adamant about it. So the officers agreed that Lieutenant Day and the other soldier, a corporal named McLaughlin, would walk to Ojo de la Vaca, procure horses or mules there, and proceed to Fort Fillmore to alert the commander of the robbery. Lieutenant Trenton and the wounded Sergeant Scott would travel on to Barney's, where

Trenton would form a posse, and Scott would travel on to alert the dragoons at Fort Aravaipa on the other side of Doubtful Cañon. Of course, by that time, Julian, Cassady, and that lot of thieves would be long gone.

"Son, I'm the only chance we have of stopping them," Trenton was telling me now. "I need your help. Which way? Did your brother tell you, give you any indication . . . ?"

"Trenton!" Marco Max yelled. "With or without you, I'm pulling out."

Cursing, the lieutenant turned away from me and climbed into the coach.

"The Janos Road!" I shouted at him, and he turned. "They'll take the Janos Road into Mexico."

The stagecoach pulled away.

"They'll head to Mexico," I told him, "then swing through Sonora into Texas."

"Thank you!"

We watched the Celerity leave, slowly. It took forever for the stagecoach to disappear. When it was out of sight, I turned, feeling Pa's stare, and looked up.

His backhand flattened me.

I don't think he meant to hit me as hard as he did, for I tasted blood in my mouth. Tears welled in my eyes, and I looked up to see Pa standing over me, fists clenched so hard his knuckles now whitened.

"Thought I taught you better. . . ." He took a deep breath, trying to regain control. Behind him, Fletcher took a step away, wetting his lips, looking worried. "The Janos Road?" Pa asked mockingly.

"I. . . ." I didn't know what to say.

"You lied to those soldiers." He pointed to our

home. I didn't know what he meant by the gesture, not right away. "You know they're not taking that road. You know exactly where they're going. Why'd you lie, Smith? How long have you known what Julian was up to? Why didn't you go with him?"

"I. . . ."

"Answer me! Answer me, and, by thunder, you'd better tell me the truth. Tell me everything. Or so help me I'll leave welts on your back and backside that'll take months to heal."

In all my years, I'd never seen Pa like this, not this angry, acting like the devil himself had taken hold of him.

"The horses," Pa said. "The horses at Alejondro's place!"

Señor Vee, lying on my bed, wounded by that barbarian half-breed. He had told Pa about the geldings left at his place.

"You put Alejondro Velásquez at risk, boy," Pa continued. "Those butchers might have murdered Alyvia, Victoria, and Dolores. You think about that, boy? Now tell me!"

"I didn't know what was going on." My confession came out more as a wail. "Jules said he and Breed were going to raise horses, sell remounts like those geldings to the Army, said that's why he wanted to leave them at *Señor* Vee's place, said you'd never let him hear the end of it if you saw that stock."

True enough, although I wonder, deep down, if I really believed that, if I knew my brother held some other motive, although I never would have guessed anything as dark as what had come about.

"I didn't know he meant to do this!"

Pa's fists unclenched, then balled again. He turned

away, stopped, looked back at me, staring with cold, cruel eyes.

"I promise," I squeaked. "It's the God's honest truth."

"The Janos Road?" He took another deep breath, releasing it like some fire-breathing dragon I'd read about in old storybooks. "You sent that fool Trenton in the opposite direction."

I couldn't look into those eyes. "Yes, sir," I mumbled.

"They left the horses at Alejondro's to change mounts. Run the stock they stole here, get fresh horses up there. Keep riding."

"Yes, sir. I guess that's what they planned."

"Good tracker would figure that. . . ." He shook his head. It didn't matter. "Why'd you lie to that soldier?"

I wiped my busted lip, and, sniffling, made myself look into Pa's eyes. "Jules," I said, "is my brother."

My emotions must have been like riding a bucking mule, jarring, unpredictable. Some times I hated Julian for all he had done. Often I wanted to fight him, maybe even kill him, for all the pain he had caused, the grief, the senseless slaughter of our livestock, our livelihood. But then . . . well . . . he was blood. My only brother, a man I had admired, loved, worshipped. I didn't want him dead.

Not yet.

That has changed as I write this, but I can't regret my decision to send Lieutenant Trenton south toward Mexico, away from Julian, Cassady, and those other murdering bandits. I still don't want the dragoons to kill Julian.

I want to do it myself. And I make this vow: I will kill him.

Pa spit and shook his head when I gave my reason. "You have no brother," he said with a bitterness I'll never forget, a bitterness I would inherit. "Get up. On your feet. You're coming with me."

He had turned to Fletcher when I slowly picked myself up, ignoring my dumb question of where we were going, speaking to the hired hand. "Fletcher, I hate to leave you like this, alone and all. Need you to tend to Alejondro. Bartolomé or Barney will be back at some point, with help. Least, I hope so. I'll also send Dolores and her girls here. They can help out."

"I'll take care of things; Mr. Munro."

"I know you will, Fletcher. You're a good hand. If the Army comes here, tell them where we're going, where Julian and the others rode. North to Alejondro's place, not south to Janos."

"Yes, sir. Where you think they'll go after they get fresh horses?"

"They ain't getting fresh horses," Pa said, and Fletcher raised his eyebrows. "But I don't know. Wouldn't make sense to ride down to Janos, and I don't think they'd ride along the Overland Trail."

"Tucson?"

"No. That Trenton's a fool if he thinks they'd go to Tucson."

Fletcher agreed, thinking aloud. "Has to be Texas, but how they'd get there . . . through the Jornado del Muerto." He shook his head. "I don't know. Reckon that gold-toothed half-breed knows some Apache trails."

"Likely," Pa said. "We'll follow them, though. As long as it takes."

Pa had shoved a revolver, belonging to one of the soldiers who had been killed, I guessed, in his waistband, and two canteens over his shoulder. He tugged his hat down low, and glanced back at me. "Let's go," he said, and I followed him, walking away from Soldier's Farewell, making our way through the night toward the Velásquez place.

We didn't speak during the first hour or so, just walked, although I wondered about the hopelessness of our pursuit. They were mounted; we were afoot. Finally I mentioned it to Pa.

"They'll be long gone," I said. "And they'll have fresh horses."

"No," he said softly. "They won't."

At that moment he stopped, unslung one of the canteens, and handed it to me. I drank greedily, hadn't realized just how thirsty I was.

"One thing you ought to learn, Smith," he said, gentler now, the rage gone as he focused on the task of steady pursuit. "Outlaws aren't smart at all. They're stupid. They're lazy." I started to return the canteen to him, then realized I should help out, carry my own. No point in Pa laboring like that, carrying everything. He took a quick sip from the other canteen, then continued talking, although now we had resumed our march.

"They think they'll find fresh mounts, but they won't. Alejondro hid them in a cañon behind his house. Hid his wife and two girls there, too. He knew Julian was up to no good, and he sure wasn't going to leave his family with a man like that half-breed killer. He waited and watched, and when the half-breed took out for Soldier's Farewell, he got the horses and his family hidden, then came to help us. So they'll run my mules and horses full out. They'll be blowing mighty hard. By now, they've already found out they've been played for the fools they are, and are having to nurse those winded animals wherever they're bound. They're cussing each other."

"They might find the horses," I suggested.

"Wouldn't have enough time. Couldn't chance it. We'll get those horses, though. How many did you say there were?"

I had to think. "Five."

"Five." He considered that a moment. "Good stock?"

"Geldings," I said. "Kind of rangy-looking. More like mustangs than the horses we got. Not as big, not as powerful as our mules or your stallions."

"Likely stolen. Any tack?"

I shook my head. "I didn't see any saddles or bridles, only halters and rope."

"Five," he said again. "We might have to ride bareback. I don't know if Alejondro has any saddles. But one of us might get a saddle. Yeah, I expect one of us will."

We kept walking.

Over the rolling hills, through arroyos, past the small forests of yucca, we kept moving, the occasional scattering of horse apples telling us we had chosen the right direction, not that any doubt had ever entered either Pa's or my mind. Dawn had broken long before we ever came to the Velásquez place, the sight of turkey buzzards circling causing my stomach to knot with fear, although Pa never stopped his stride until we crested the hill overlooking the small *jacal*, corral, and outbuildings.

Carefully he drew the revolver, and eased back the hammer. Crouching behind a twisted yucca, we must have waited a good ten, 15 minutes before he felt satisfied, then told me to follow him, and we started down the hill, revolver still cocked, water sloshing inside our canteens.

A coyote bolted out of the open door to *Señor* Vee's house. Above us, the buzzards waited patiently. Pa didn't seem concerned, and he walked straight into the house. He was kneeling over the body by the time I caught up with him, holding something in his left hand that I didn't recognize at first, the Colt revolver now back inside his waistband.

Those ruffians had ransacked the house, and I could just picture their frustrations, finding, as Pa had said, no fresh horses waiting for them. I hadn't expected them to kill anyone, though. Pa had said they'd be cussing each other, but they'd done a sight more than that. They'd started killing each other.

Ben Jakes sat propped up against the wall beside the fireplace, mouth open but eyes closed, hands still resting against his stomach where one of the bullets had entered. Another had pierced his heart.

Now, I've never tried to hide my contempt for that no-account. He had betrayed us, joining Cassady's lot, a Judas, but I can't say I wanted to see him dead, not really.

"Why'd they kill him?" I asked Pa.

"Five horses," Pa said. "They never planned on keeping him around."

Five horses. For Julian, Breed, Pinto, Howell, and Cassady. Pa had it figured all this time.

"But there were no remounts here."

Pa rose. "No," was all he said. He held the book,

which had been in his left hand, out toward me, and I blinked, not believing, then snatched the diary. My diary!

"Must have dropped it," Pa said, "accidentally."

My head bobbed in agreement, but I'll never be sure it had been an accident. I think Julian left it behind for me, on purpose. For forgiveness? Well, if that were his reason, he'll be disappointed, for I can never forgive him. Not even for Ben Jakes. I looked at the body again.

"There was no reason to shoot him," I said.

"No," he said again. "There wasn't. But they didn't need him any more." He sighed. "Took his mule, though. I'd hoped they would have left it behind. Come on. Let's get him out of Dolores's *casa*. No need for her and the girls to see this."

It wasn't fitting, the burial we gave Ben Jakes, but I didn't have much to work with, and Pa ordered me not to spend too much time and muscle on the likes of him. The only tools I had were a garden hoe and my own hands, but I went to work on the side of the hill, away from the house, while Pa walked to the cañon to fetch Tori, her sister, and her ma, and the horses. I carved out a shallow hole for Ben Jakes, rolled him into it, and managed to get some of that hill to slide over him, then piled what rocks I could find atop the shallow grave. By the time I'd finished, Pa had returned, and I have to admit relief swept over my whole body when I saw Tori and the others. Coming over the hill, I dropped my hoe, and ran out to greet them, hugged Tori something tight, then Alyvia, then, crying now, I hugged *Señora* Dolores.

"I'm sorry," I told her. "I'm sorry about everything."

"Is all right," she said tightly, struggling with the

English. "We fine, Smith. *Muy bien*. God has taken care of us."

Somehow, I managed to nod, and stepped away, damming the tears, wetting my lips, but then I looked at Alyvia, saw the tears flowing down her cheeks, and I wanted to say something, wanted to apologize for Julian, wanted to say I know how she felt, her heart breaking, feeling betrayed, but our reunion had to be short. We had to go on, after Julian and his friends, and Tori and Alyvia were needed with their father lying wounded at Soldier's Farewell.

Five horses. After filling our canteens in the well, we rode two piebalds, bareback and with hackamores, while Pa let *Señora* Dolores and her daughters take the other three geldings back to the stagecoach station. Tori carried my diary. I asked her to return it to Soldier's Farewell. It contained the descriptions of Cassady and the others, which might come in handy for the law, and I didn't really have a way to carry the book with me.

Besides, I told myself, I'd have no need of it, not where I was going.

Where were we going?

Texas lay east, a hot ride on worn-out mules, but the trail led us northwest, eventually intersecting a well-used road and following it toward the mountains. Maybe they planned on leaving the road at some point. After all, I had heard of a route through the Mimbres Mountains, up toward Fort Craig on the Río Grande, but, then, I couldn't see them going that way. Santa Fé? Why would they go north? Yet if they kept traveling this direction, they'd wind up among the Navajos. By jingo, already we found ourselves deep in Apache country, with Red Sleeves himself on the prod. Maybe they planned on turning back, going south, perhaps to Tucson after all, or finding Cooke's Wagon Road or the Janos Road and making their way into Mexico.

But, no, they moved northwest, making no attempt to hide their tracks.

"I don't understand this," I told Pa as we watered our horse in a hidden pool. "There's no reason for them to go this way."

"No?"

"This road don't go nowhere," I said, before remembering Julian's school lessons in spite of myself. "Anywhere, I mean. Doesn't go anywhere, I mean."

"No?"

Tugging on the hackamore, he pulled his pinto gelding away, and let the horse carry him back up the road.

"Then why'd they build a road?" he said once I caught up. Pa was toying with me, testing me.

"Well, it goes to Burchville, I reckon." I'd never been there, but had heard plenty of stories and met a few folks on there way to or from the camps and mines in those mountains. "The Pinos Altos mines."

"Uhn-huh."

I studied on this for 5 minutes. With a furrowed brow, I asked: "You reckon there are . . . ?" I had to remember the term. "You reckon there are Southern sympathizers at those mines? You reckon they're going to turn over the money they stole to Confederate officials there?"

Now Pa's brow knotted, and he reined in the pinto, looked me in the eye, and said: "That money was never meant for the South, Son."

"But. . . ." No, he couldn't be right. "But Julian . . . but Cassady. . . ."

"First of all, I know Jefferson Davis and I know

Wade Hampton." He kicked the horse into a walk, and I followed. "Know both of them, I reckon, as well as I do any man, especially Wade. They would have no part in a robbery such as this. I will grant you that there are many Southern fire-eaters . . . what's that they call them, Southrons? Well, sure I'll bet my bottom dollar you'll find many of those praying for war. But not Jeff. Certainly not Wade. Not many of them, I warrant. They want to leave the Union peaceful. This was robbery, an act of greed, not an act of war. Wade would never back anything like this. No righteous man would."

"Cassady said he was a soldier."

Pa spit. "Smith, I've seen soldiers. Was a soldier once. Cassady ain't got the makings. Nor does that half-breed, and certainly not Howell, probably not Pinto. They ain't nothing but a pack of thieves."

"And . . . ?" I couldn't mention my brother's name.

"You ever heard the word hornswoggled?"

"Yes, sir."

"Know what it means?"

"Kind of like you got fooled."

"Right. I think Cassady hornswoggled Ju-. . . ." His lips tightened. He couldn't say the name, either.

I thought about this as we rode, trying to get everything worked out in my mind. Julian's a Union officer at Fort Tejon, but he's Southern-born, probably knows he must follow South Carolina and Mississippi, his home states as they were, or maybe Missouri. I remember when he had been arguing with Pa, trying to explain why he had joined Cassady. What do you want me to do? Fight the friends and family we had back in Camden and Port Gibson? Fight Ma's relations?

So Cassady had gotten to know Julian, gotten close

to him, learning of his work at Fort Tejon. Cassady had planned the robbery, and had hornswoggled my brother, preyed on his Southern ties. Julian thought this was a strike for the new Confederacy, when in reality it was a strike for Cassady's pockets. Maybe that's why they had really killed Ben Jakes. They just didn't want to split the money with him.

During the robbery, they had announced to everyone their plans, to raise money for the Confederacy, to let the Army think they would go to Texas, somehow, even if by way of Mexico, maybe to turn in the money to the treasury at Montgomery, Alabama. That way, the Army would look south for the robbers, concentrating on the Mexican and Texas borders. Even I had sent that fool Lieutenant Trenton toward the Janos Road. No one would think to look in Burchville. Or maybe they'd go on from the mines. To the mining camps in Colorado Territory, or even as far away as San Francisco.

Robbers! Not partisan soldiers.

Pa was right. They had hornswoggled Julian.

No, I thought, if Julian wanted no part of robbery, if he had thought this had been for the Southern cause, if he had not been fooled, then why were we following his tracks to Pinos Altos? Why hadn't he stopped them from killing Ben Jakes? Why hadn't they killed him, too? Something else troubled me, too, as I thought about Pa's theory.

"Why bother to change mounts?" I asked. "It ain't that far to the mines, is it?"

He considered this for maybe a quarter mile. Maybe he hadn't reasoned everything out, but at last he shook his head. "Stolen mules would give them away in Burchville," he said. "Folks might recognize the brand. Maybe these geldings weren't stolen, after all. And changing horses would make the Army, the law, maybe even me, think they had planned on going far, taking a long way to Texas. Besides, by the time anyone thought to look in the mines, there would be no tracks to follow." I wasn't that sure Pa was following any tracks by now anyway, just going along the road, in no particular hurry. "But I warrant we'll find them in Burchville."

The weather turned cooler, downright cold, and the country changed, too, as the road climbed upward, leaving creosote and saltbush behind, the yucca making way for Gambel oak and mahogany. We had stopped talking now, both of us deep in thought, I'd guess, riding along in silence, hearing nothing but the clopping of hoofs. I let my gelding fall in behind Pa, wet my lips, and must have drifted off to sleep.

My head jerked up, and I realized we had stopped. Blinking away sleep, I started to say something, but Pa raised a hand, and I knew he wanted me to keep quiet. His revolver was out, thumb on the hammer, and he watched carefully.

Here the road forked, the branch to the left trailing alongside the beginning of the mountain range, crossing a sandy arroyo up ahead, shady, and it sure looked like a good place to take a nap and slake my thirst for I could hear a brook bubbling somewhere in that little wood. The road to the right would go into the mountains. I had to think about this. Left went on to Burchville and Pinos Altos, I determined, while right took travelers to Santa Rita, where I guess men have been digging for copper since before Pa was even born, with Mexicans hauling the stuff down to Chihuahua City and Indians finding the stuff long before that. Fact is, copper had been drawing men to these parts for what seemed like forever until they discovered gold at Pinos Altos back in '59. Then it struck me that maybe Pa hadn't figured everything out just right, that maybe I had been correct.

Julian and the others could have turned right, taken the old road to Santa Rita, not Burchville, and then followed that trail through the Mimbres Mountains all the way to the Río Grande. Shoot, that made a whole lot more sense than hitting Burchville. Nobody would think to look for them going that way. Sure, it would prove risky, what with the Apaches acting up, but those same Indians would scare off much pursuit—and Julian had that half-breed with them. By grab, they might have even made a deal with the Apaches to let them pass through peaceable. Now, I didn't know a whole lot about the country northeast of here, but it struck me from what I did know that once they reached the Río Grande near Fort Craig, they could cut across the Jornado del Muerto all the way to the Pecos River, then just follow the Pecos south to Texas.

Mr. Fletcher had even suggested they might cross the Jornado, especially if Breed knew the trails, the water holes. Not many white men would venture pursuit through that rough country.

"They split up," Pa said at last.

"Which way do we go?" I asked him.

Sighing, Pa shoved the revolver into his waistband, clucked at his horse, and turned right. We started into the mountains toward the copper mines.

I've always wondered why we chose that path. Pa had seem jo-fired on going to Burchville, but, with little comment, he turned toward the copper mines.

Maybe he figured Julian went this way, or maybe he thought Julian had gone to Burchville, and, deep down, he really didn't want to meet up with his oldest son.

I never got a chance to ask him about it. Not sure he would have answered me.

Pa reined up again, but this time slid off the horse, handing me the hackamore and telling me in a hoarse whisper to wait here. Crouching, he moved a few rods and braced himself against a large boulder, revolver cocked, studying what must have been an old camping place just up the road.

Well, I could see what vexed him so. A mule stood in the shade at the edge of that clearing, drinking water and grazing. One of our mules, old Hampton, still saddled, still bridled, the reins dragging on the ground at that old sorrel jack's feet.

Ben Jakes's mount! Or this mule had played out and one of the outlaw's had taken old Ben's. The jack just stood there, oblivious to us, and my pinto started getting ticklish, wanting to join the mule in that pasture, wanted to get his fill of water. He didn't have Pa's patience. A branch snapped, and I saw what else must have troubled Pa.

A saddled mare walked over from the forest, its reins also trailing, stopped, and drank. Well, I'd know that mare anywhere, for Pa had brung her with us when we left Missouri. He liked breeding that horse, who had been the dam of many of our best mules.

For what must have been 20 minutes, Pa just stood there, watching, studying, waiting, while I struggled to keep my gelding in place while holding onto Pa's. Finally he let out a heavy sigh, and looked at me.

"You see anything?"

I couldn't believe he was asking me, and I felt mighty proud—at least, right then—and shook my head. "Just Molly and Hampton," I answered. "You reckon they both gave out?"

"Could be," he said, whispering, still not convinced. "One of them might be riding double now."

A chill raced up my backbone. They had killed Ben Jakes because they didn't have enough horses. They might have killed Julian for the same reason here. He could be lying in those woods.

"Could be they had more horses waiting for them here," Pa said. "Could be anything." He went back to scouting, listening, watching, but only for 5 more minutes, then he looked back at me and said: "Wait here." Slowly he stepped onto the road, and cautiously began making his way down the road to the clearing, his revolver sweeping across one way, then the other, toward the woods, up into the hills, down the road, even behind us.

He hadn't gone 15 yards before the first shot rang out.

His scream roared above the pounding echoes of the gunfire, and I caught a glimpse of him falling, dropping his revolver, unfired, but that's all I saw. I had my hands full trying to keep my seat as that pinto started pitching and snorting. I dropped the hackamore's to Pa's mount, and that horse took off for parts unknown, heading down the road to the fork. My teeth like to about broke in half, and I grabbed a fistful of mane, but I was bareback, and that mustang was scared and angry, so I didn't keep my seat for long. The gelding landed, then bucked high, lowering his head, and I went flying, losing my hold on the hackamore, yelling as that boulder rushed out to greet me.

It's a miracle I didn't break my neck, but all I came away with was a bloody nose. I bounced off the boulder and landed on my backside, crashing hard, but I pulled myself up in a hurry, as another gunshot drowned out the pounding of hoofs as our horses bolted away.

"Pa!"

He lay writhing. Another bullet hit him, rolling him over, and he groaned and cursed.

I started for him.

"Stay . . . back!" I don't know how he could even manage to speak, but I didn't listen. A bullet tugged at my shirt, and I grabbed his shoulders, tried to drag him back toward that boulder, but Pa's a mighty big man, and I didn't have the muscles even to budge him.

Something hard bashed the back of my head, and I went sprawling on the dirt, away from Pa, my head just swimming as I landed, stunned, but conscious, and recognizing that cruel voice.

"*Mi amigo.*"

Breed!

Opening my eyes, I saw Breed press the foot of his moccasin under Pa's stomach, and roll him over. "*Adiós,*" he said, and aimed a double-action Kerr revolver in his right hand. In his left, he held a revolving rifle.

He had been waiting for us all that time. Waiting to kill us. I guess that was his plan, although I don't know how long he planned on waiting on the road. Maybe Cassady paid him extra for this duty as a rear guard.

He'd never collect.

I shot him in the thigh.

I'd landed beside the cocked pistol Pa had dropped.

Perhaps Breed thought he had knocked me cold, when he split my head open with the barrel of his .45, but I reached out, grabbed the weapon, pointed, and pulled the trigger.

Pa and the others never had let me pull guard duty or anything like that, and I couldn't really blame them. I wasn't much of a hand with a pistol, and it had to be luck that my first shot struck Breed at all.

"Mother of God!" he said, staggering away from Pa, dropping the rifle but still holding the Kerr, seeing me sprawled out, smoke rising from the barrel. He spread his legs, raised his pistol, and I used my left hand to cock the revolver, then steady my aim. Breed pulled the trigger first, but, instead of a roar, I heard only a small pop, knew his gun had misfired.

Mine didn't.

But I missed.

He pulled the trigger again. Another misfire. No, he was empty, and he flung the revolver at me in rage, then whipped a knife from his sheath, and started limping toward me. I had cocked the gun again, closed my eyes, knew I was dead, and pulled the trigger.

I would have missed him that time, too, or maybe, with God's luck, I might have wounded him, but Pa reached out and tripped him, so, instead, the bullet smashed into the top of his head, and Breed fell in the dirt, dead before he hit the ground.

Pulling myself up, leaving the smoking revolver on the dirt, I raced to Pa, tried not to look at the man I had just killed. I fell at Pa's side, tears blinding both of us, tried to think of what I could do, how I could help him.

"Listen to me," he said.

My head bobbed. Blood dripped down my hair, into my shirt.

"You gotta get . . . me some . . . help."

He had been shot in the left arm, between the wrist and elbow, and again in his left side.

"We'll get out of here, Pa," I told him. I looked up, but Molly the mare and Hampton the mule had taken off during the shooting, too, loping up the road toward Santa Rita.

"Santa Rita . . . closer," Pa said. "Get . . . help."

"I ain't leaving you!"

"You got . . . to."

With his help, I managed to get him off the road and to the camping ground, propping him up against an oak tree near the little stream. I bathed his wounds, plugged the hole in his side, and started wrapping a bandanna over the bad hole in his arm. He screamed in pain, and I fought back tears, nausea. The bone was broken, broken bad, part of it sticking out of the skin.

"Best . . . hurry," he said. I'd never seen him so pale. I knew he was right. I had to leave him, had to get help, or he'd die. Looking back on it, I think he knew he was dying then, and didn't want me to see him die like that, in such horrible pain.

"I'll get help!" I leaped up.

"Smith," he said. "I shouldn't . . . have hit . . . you. Back . . . at Soldier's . . . Farewell. Wasn't . . . your fault."

"Yes, it was," I told him, and, ignoring my pounding, bleeding head, sprinted toward the copper mines.

Pa didn't die.

Fooled the doctor, he did. Fooled *Señora* Dolores. Even fooled me.

Fearing I'd never see Pa alive again, I raced up the pike, but had gone scarcely three miles before I ran into a bunch of Mexican traders heading down from the copper mines. In broken Spanish, I pleaded for their help, and they understood the bulk of what I was trying to say, so they hurried on down, and we found Pa where I'd left him. The leader was an old man, and he said they had a *bruja* traveling with them, his sister, a wrinkled old crone who started making a poultice and chanting some song while the white-haired gentleman built a fire and spoke softly to my father, who by this time kept drifting in and out of consciousness. The old man said something to one of his men, and that *hombre* disappeared behind one of the carts, then came back with a hand saw.

"You ain't . . . ?" I started to cry again.

The old Mexican spoke sympathetically, his head firm, nodding as he told me what I guess I already knew. He was right. This had to be done.

I won't write down all that happened. Just don't want to relive it. They sawed off Pa's left arm at the elbow. Deep down, I expected the shock to kill him. So did the old man and his sister, but once they tied off the arteries, got that bleeding stopped, got the bullet out of his side and that hole patched up, they loaded Pa onto the back of an ox-drawn cart, and we started down the road. They were Christian folks, mighty good to us, and I can never thank them enough. Certainly can't repay them, and they deserved a whole lot more than Breed's revolving rifle that I forced on them as payment. Going to Janos, they said, but they went by the Velásquez home, though it was out of their way, and left Pa and me there. I didn't think Pa had enough strength to make it all the way to Soldier's Farewell.

For a couple of days, there was just Pa and me, for I couldn't find the courage to leave him alone, what with him half out of his head, speaking to Ma, sweating, likely dying. As if answering my prayers, though, *Señora* Dolores returned, and she took over the doctoring. Tori and Alyvia came home, too, with their father, weak but alive, and growing stronger. I can't write enough praise for Tori's mother, either—how she tended those two wounded men, can't applaud Tori and Alyvia for all their help. So Pa and *Señor* Vee kept improving, and *Señor* Vee said I'd become a man. After a week, I took Pa home.

Mr. Barney fetched a doctor from La Mesilla, and that pill-roller said Pa'd eventually die, but that was a week ago, and Pa's up and around, barking orders. One of the first things he did, and one of the last things for the Overland, was post a letter on the Eastbound. I don't know who he wrote, but he was up half the night composing it, alternating between writing a few words and taking a few sips of mescal.

He has taken more to drink. Don't know if that is brought on by pitying himself, hating Julian, numbing the pain from his wounds, or lamenting the loss of the Overland job.

The Overland has stopped. Moving north, but we really knew that would happen once Texas left the Union. The last coach came through right after the Mesilla doctor checked on Pa. So we've said good bye to Mr. Barney, Mr. Fletcher—hate to see him go. Bartolomé's staying, not with us, but working over at the Velásquez place. Emmett Mills plans on sticking around at Cooke's Spring, too, with a handful of others, but most of the Overland crews are parting ways, either taking jobs with the Overland up north, on the Central Route, or going home, to get ready for the war that's coming. Marco Max said farewell, said he'd be going back to Vermont to preserve the Union, if need be.

Pa's not going with the Overland, though. We're staying put. Don't know what we're going to do.

Tori and her ma came by today, and while *Señora* Dolores looked after the stump of Pa's arm, Tori asked me why we'd stay here after all that had happened. Oh, she said, she'd enjoy it much if I were to stay here. It would fill her heart with much happiness, she said, and she took my hand into hers.

I didn't answer her. Couldn't. I didn't want to break her heart. I know why we're staying here. Pa's waiting on Julian to come home. So am I.

So I can kill him.

April 2, 1861

I don't write in this book the way I once did. Don't like the memories. Wind's blowing like a gale tonight, and Pa's drunk again. Seems that's all he does of late. Maybe Tori and her ma were right. This place is cursed.

Found the diary beside my bed while I was looking for a rag to clean my revolver after killing a rabbit for supper. When those Mexican traders were working on Pa, cutting off his arm, some others buried Breed in that camping spot where he had ambushed us, and they brought me his revolving rifle and the double-action revolver. I gave the old man, the leader, the rifle, insisted he take it as payment for all he had done, but I kept the Kerr .45. It's English-made, a five-shot, and I keep it well-oiled.

It's the gun I plan on using to kill Julian.

April 21, 1861

Well, the war has started. The fire-eaters in Charleston, South Carolina torched their cannons and started shelling Fort Sumter. We got news yesterday from some dragoons came through, bound for Fort Yuma. The bombardment on Sumter started on April 12, and the Union soldiers held out for as long as they could—brave lads, they were—but in less than two days, it was all over.

Wonder if Julian was there.

April 25, 1861

More visitors today, but I'd just as soon never have seen these. They were soldiers, too, with the grim task of digging up Captain Ulf Beckenbauer. His relations want to bury him back home in Chester County, Pennsylvania. Pa and I walked with the soldiers down the little trail to the burial ground.

"Which one is it?" a sunburned corporal asked, and pointed. "That one?"

"No," Pa said softly. I wonder if he knew for certain, in his cups as he was. "That one."

Four graves I saw, and did some ciphering in my head. The German captain had been killed, and two of the couriers. Yet there was another grave, older, and it struck me odd that I'd never noticed it before. As much exploring as I'd done around here, I hadn't realized someone had been buried here. Well, there was no marker, or at least there hadn't been one for ages, just a mound of rocks, and many of them scattered about over time.

"Pa?" I asked hesitantly. "Who else is buried here?"

He sighed. "You need us for anything else?" he called out to the corporal.

"No, sir."

We walked away, and when we got back to the old station home, Pa uncorked a keg of mescal and shook his head. "That's how this place got its name, Smith. Dragoons were camped here years ago. Story goes one of the soldiers woke up one morning, just ran out, called out good bye to his friends, put a revolver against the side of his head, pulled the trigger."

I swallowed. "You mean . . . he killed himself?"

"Yeah. Must have gone insane. The wind . . . this country . . . it can drive a strong man mad."

"And that's why Tori and her ma . . . why they think this place is cursed, why they never will spend the night here?"

"I suppose." He lifted the jug and drank. "Soldier's Farewell. Some farewell, eh?"

May 15, 1861

"Pa!"

I stood out by the stable, had been there a while after I spotted the dust. I'd been feeding the mules. Our mules. Pa had bought two jacks and a jenny from the Overland before the company moved to the Central Route, and *Señor* Vee had tracked down Hampton and Molly the mare, tracked them all the way to the Pinos Altos mines once he got back on his feet, so we have five animals. Not that we ever go anywhere much, except when I'll go hunting us up something to eat.

He came out of the house, pulling the suspenders

over his shoulders, and staggered out to see what the commotion was about. He squinted, his vision blurred from the mescal he had been drinking for breakfast.

"One rider," he said. "Ain't no Apache."

"No, sir."

Recognizing the animal, same as I did, Pa went straight as a flagpole. "Get inside, Smith," he told me, and I was mightily glad of the order. I left him waiting to greet our visitor, while I darted inside to fetch the Kerr .45.

It's hard to write how I really felt when the rider reined up on that wonderful Tobiano mule. I came outside ready to kill my brother, but stopped in my tracks, feeling foolish holding a heavy revolver while Pa patted Sweet Ainsley's neck and invited the bearded miner to light down and have a whiskey.

"Mighty neighborly of you," the stranger said. "Was hopin' you could spare some water, but John Barleycorn would taste even better."

"Smith!" Pa called to me. "Feed and water this man's mule."

The man called himself Jesse Holden, and, after a few drinks, said he had bought the mule in Burchville. He was giving up on striking it rich, wanted to go back home to his ma's place south of Fort Lancaster in Texas. New Mexico Territory, Arizona Territory, whatever you wanted to call it, just wasn't safe with Red Sleeves and Cochise riled up and butchering any white man or Mexican they could find.

"Burchville," Pa said.

Remembering how we had tracked Julian and his pards, I felt foolish. "They split up," I reminded Pa.

"You said so, remember? Split up. Some went to Santa Rita, others to Burchville. We never went to Burchville."

Holden, ignoring us, helped himself to Pa's jug.

"One." Pa stroked his rough beard. "One man rode to Burchville. I'd forgotten."

"So did I. Just wanted to take care of you."

By the time Pa had beat away the devil or death, I figured Julian, Cassady, Howell, and Pinto were long gone. After all, the soldiers looking for them never cut any trail, and, after a month or so, they gave up that money as lost.

"He wouldn't still be up there," I said.

Pa studied on it. "Might find something about him, though," he said.

"About who?" Holden asked.

Pa ignored him, sober of a sudden, but I decided to answer the question. Maybe Holden knew something.

"The man who sold you that mule," I said.

He snorted. "Quinn Nation? Runs the livery."

"Nation?" My first thought, or hope, was that Julian had changed his name, had used his share of the money to buy a livery, but then I realized the truth of it all. Julian had sold Sweet Ainsley, had bought another mount, had ridden out of Burchville months ago.

"Maybe Mr. Nation knows where he went," Pa said. A long bet, for certain.

"Who?" Holden asked.

"The gent who sold that mule to your livery man," Pa said.

Holden blinked. "You got a right heavy interest in that old mule," he said.

"I do," Pa said. "Fact is, I'd like to buy her off you.

Got a pretty good mare in the stable who'll get you across Texas a whole lot quicker than a pinto mule."

"Criminy." Holden smiled drunkenly. "If that hoss'll walk, you got yourself a deal. Ain't fittin' for a white man to be ridin' a pinto. And that mule is bad luck. That's how come I got her cheap from Quinn Nation."

"How'd Nation get her?" I asked impatiently.

Holden looked at me as if I were the dumbest man on earth, as if everyone had heard what had happened in February in Burchville.

"He killed the man who rode in on her," Holden said.

May 16, 1861

We're back from Burchville, a wasted trip in some ways—not that I expected to find Julian up there, or even his grave. Pa traded Holden for Sweet Ainsley, and, as soon as that drunken Texican rode off on Molly, we saddled up and rode for the mine country.

Quinn Nation didn't have much to say about the man he had killed in a saloon, even after I tried my best to convince him we had no interest in avenging the man's death or demanding a coroner's inquest.

"He was cheatin' at cards," Nation finally sang out. "Would have killed me if his pistol hadn't misfired."

"Catch his name?" Pa asked.

"Never give one. Buried him in the cemetery." Bitterly he shook his head. "I had to pay for the funeral."

"Young man?" I asked. "Dark-haired? Had a mustache? Looked a bit like me?"

The livery man splattered tobacco juice against the wall. "Not hardly. Big man, right big, and ugly as sin. Had a patch over one of his eyes and a terrible scar." With a thick finger, Nation traced a line from one cheek, over the nose, and onto the other cheek.

Pa and I looked at each other. Howell. The cold-blooded Texas man-killer.

"He have any money on him?" Pa asked.

It took Nation a while to answer. "Just enough to buy in the game."

He wasn't much of a liar, but I didn't press him. Quinn Nation wore brand-new boots, a silk hat, brocade vest with a silver chain hooked onto a William Johnson watch. I remembered that watch, could picture Howell taking the timepiece, chain, and elk-tooth fob off the man from Ohio, along with his money belt, during the robbery at Soldier's Farewell. New duds? A solid gold London-made watch? Quinn Nation dressed too well for a Burchville livery man. I don't think he spent his own money to bury Howell, either, but it didn't matter.

Howell was six feet under, while Cassady, Pinto, and my brother had ridden on to Santa Rita and, most likely, out of New Mexico Territory.

July 30, 1861

Sad news to report. Emmett Mills is dead. From what *Señor* Vee says, poor Emmett and six others were attacked by Apaches at Cooke's Spring, had tried to escape in an abandoned stagecoach, but the warriors cut all seven of them down. This was the work of Red Sleeves. Emmett was a good man, and *Señor* Vee suggests that it is no longer safe for us to remain at Soldier's Farewell. After killing Emmett and the others, the Indians burned the station, and that's too close to home for *Señor* Vee, who is bound for La Mesilla with his family and Bartolomé until the Apache troubles are over.

Pa refuses to retreat. He says Red Sleeves and Cochise will leave us alone.

We also have heard of a big battle in the East. Confederate soldiers have whipped the Union Army near Manassas, Virginia. Southern sympathizers are dancing in the streets of Mesilla, saying the war will be over in a week.

September 4, 1861

A letter came today. *Señor* Vee brought it from Mesilla. It's from Wade Hampton, now commanding a legion or something in the Confederate Army. Hampton was wounded at Manassas, but that's the only part of the letter Pa mentioned. I asked Pa if Senator Hampton wrote any news of Julian, but Pa never answered me. He merely thanked *Señor* Vee for bringing the letter, which he burned in the fireplace.

December 25, 1861

Christmas. Yet I feel Jesus has abandoned us.

January 2, 1862

A new year. No news from the war. No news from Tori Velásquez. No news from anywhere.

February 5, 1862

I remember Pa always telling me how the war would never touch us in New Mexico Territory, but the war has come here. Cassady even predicted it back when he was robbing the Fort Tejon payroll, and now a Confederate general named Sibley has invaded the territory. He has an army of 20,000 men, we are told, with plans to capture Santa Fé and go on up to the Colorado mines and take that gold for the Confederacy.

Heavy traffic on the road, much more than recently. Some Rebel soldiers rode through here on their way to Tucson, and we have learned that Union troops are marching from California to stop these invaders.

February 25, 1861

More news of a major battle on the Río Grande near Fort Craig. The Confederate Army has defeated Colonel Canby at Valverde. 1,000s of dead have turned the river red.

Pa took the report silently, and stayed awake all night. He woke me this morning—sober . . . he hasn't been drinking at all—and said we needed to saddle up. "We're riding out."

"Where?" I asked him.

"Valverde."

I let that sink in. "What for?"

"To see if Julian's there. Dead or alive."

Shaking the sleep out of my brain, I couldn't believe it. "Pa," I said. "That don't . . . that doesn't make a lick of sense. Those troops came from Texas. Julian's off fighting with Wade Hampton back East."

"No." He sounded more like the old Pa, determined, right, a mountain. "He ain't with Hampton. Get up."

April 18, 1862

Back home. We never should have left. While we were gone, Apaches stole the stock we left behind, tore down the stable, wrecked our home, but they didn't burn us out.

A forlorn hope. That's what this trip was.

Well, we did learn a few things. First of all, Sibley's army didn't number any 20,000. It was more like 2,500, and 1,000s were not killed at Valverde. Doubt if they buried more than 200.

We didn't locate Julian. I never once thought we would, but Pa must have hoped we would have found him, dead or alive. A Union captain at Fort Craig took us to the post hospital, where we, to my shock, found Lieutenant Day—can't recall his first name, though it's probably written down in this book—badly wounded. He had lost both eyes from canister, and the captain said a stomach wound would prove mortal. For the life of me, I can never figure out how Pa recognized that dying mess that had once been a man, had once been a friend to my brother.

Pa sat by the bed, whispering, telling the dragoon he would be all right. I leaned against the wall, hating the smell of the place, staring silently, mouth open, unbelieving.

"Did you see my . . . son?" Pa asked at length.

"Julian wasn't here, sir," Day replied weakly. "You know he wasn't."

"Well. . . ."

"It wasn't his fault," Day said when Pa rose, and Pa just looked down on that blind, dying man, looked down on him with pity, or was it curiosity or contempt? "He followed his heart."

Having heard enough, I turned to leave.

"I've forgiven him," Day said. "You should, too."

Sibley's troops kept on going north, capturing Albuquerque, then Santa Fé, and went right on, marching, bound for victory at Fort Union, the Rebs figured, but they never got that far. From what we hear down south, the Confederates turned back another Union force at Glorieta Pass, but some Colorado volunteers under command of a major named Chivington struck the supply train, wiped out the whole train, so the Rebels are hightailing it back to Texas.

Seems like the war's over in New Mexico Territory.

August 4, 1862

The last of the California Column came through the other day, bound for old Fort Thorn on the Río Grande.

Union volunteers have been moving down the road for about a month, chasing those Texas Confederates who have been out of the territory since spring. I wouldn't write much about this, on account that I see this book is almost filled up, but the commander of the troops stopped by to talk to Pa.

He's General Carleton. I remember when Julian

served under him at Fort Tejon, he was just a captain with the dragoons. Didn't like Carleton much. He said he wanted to personally thank Pa and me for all we had done trying to stop the payroll robbery last year, said had he known of Julian's treachery, he should have killed him back when they were chasing the Paiutes. He started to curse Julian, called him a yellow dog, and that's when Pa sobered up, and told him to withdraw those comments or they'd get shoved down his throat, said Julian was his son, following his heart, and, by thunder, no body ever called a Munro a coward.

That struck me as odd, and Carleton rode out of here madder than a bee-stung bear, but I reckon he wasn't half as riled as me. As Pa poured two fingers of mescal in his coffee mug, now that he was drinking again, I asked him: "Since when do you defend Jules?"

"He's a Munro. He's your brother."

With a snort, I cursed Julian and Pa.

That's only the second time I can recollect Pa hitting me, not spanking me or giving me a good whipping as a kid, but knocking me to the floor. Split my lip, but I've grown some, and haven't been living on mescal, so I jumped right back up, balled my fists, and almost struck back.

"You once told me I didn't have a brother!" I shouted. "And I don't." Turning, because I knew the tears would flow soon, I stormed outside, stopped, and pointed my finger at Pa. "And don't you ever hit me again."

August 15, 1862

Still not on speaking terms with Pa.

September 3, 1862

Things back to normal at Soldier's Farewell. I do the hunting and cooking, hire out for a couple of days, sometimes in Mowry City or Burchville, to earn enough for flour or beans, powder and lead. Pa gets drunk on mescal, which he trades for or begs from travelers, even Apaches. We're talking again. Just don't have much to say.

December 1, 1862

Just realized my birthday has passed again without notice. I'm 14. I probably would not have even re-membered but a man on a jackass brought a letter today from La Mesilla, a letter from Tori Velásquez, who wished me much happiness, said she missed me, and shared some news. Alyvia is to marry Bar-tolomé Diego Chavez y Chavez—never knew his full name till this letter came—at the San Albino Church on the plaza at La Mesilla on Christmas Eve, and she, her sister, and her parents would be honored if could pull ourselves away from business and come to the wedding.

Business. That made me laugh.

Yet it would be nice to see Tori, talk to *Señor* Vee, eat some of *Señora* Dolores's good grub, but I can never leave Soldier's Farewell. It's like the curse has anchored me here, and Pa, waiting for Julian's return.

February 10, 1863

Old Red Sleeves, Mangas Coloradas, is dead. A couple of soldiers stopped by today for water, said they were carrying a dispatch from Fort McLane to Fort Union, although I suspected they were deserters lighting out to Pinos Altos.

"Killed tryin' to escape," one of the bluecoats said, and laughed and laughed till tears ran down into his beard.

"Came in for a peace parley," the other soldier said, "that Apache butcher did, but we took him captive, then Gen'ral West, he says to us . . . 'Men, that ol' murderer has left a bloody trail stretchin' 500 miles. I want him dead come tomorrow morn.'

"So Harv and me heat up our bayonets, you see, put 'em under than old redskin's feet, and he's a tough ol' coot, but he finally sits up and shouts for us to quit tormentin' him so." Their laughter turned my stomach. "And that's when the boys shot him to pieces."

"Tryin' to escape," the other soldier said.

I was glad to see them go. Not because they were a couple of vermin, but because somehow I sort of understood Julian's feelings. I kept hearing those words he yelled at Pa all those months ago.

You told me before I left for the Academy about duty, about honor, but I think I left all that at Fort Tejon. We went after those Paiutes, Pa, because Captain Carleton said they had killed some settlers. But those Indians had nothing to do with those killings, Pa. Carleton knew that. Colonel Dawson knew it. We all knew it, but we still pursued the Paiutes. We killed a lot of them. For what? Nothing. Nothing but glory for Dawson and Carleton. Because nobody cares if an Indian is innocent. You want me to fight for that?

It doesn't matter, though. I'll still kill Julian when he returns.

March 12, 1863

Julian's birthday today. Wonder where he is.

July 19, 1863

Word comes of great Union victories in Pennsylvania and at Vicksburg, Mississippi. Also, the Velásquez family has returned to their home, what with the murder of Red Sleeves. Well, the newlyweds, Alyvia and Bartolomé, remain in La Mesilla, where Bartolomé is working at a livery stable. *Señora* Dolores commented on how much I have grown, while I just kept staring at Tori. She looks like an angel, and I forgot all those memories of her as a kid, pestering me to death.

Señor Vee, he looks much older, and needs a cane to get around good, and that's when I found myself staring at Pa, and realizing just how much he has aged. Hardly any meat on him. Part of that's from the liquor, but we've been living off varmints I can shoot, and beans. His beard is unruly, practically halfway down his chest, and although they'd never say anything rude, I know the stink of both Pa and me offended Tori and her folks. We invited them to spend the night, but, naturally, they refused.

Nighttime now. They're long gone. Wind's howling.

October 3, 1863

Pa's dying. Found him this morning slumped over the table, jug overturned, mescal spilled all over the floor. I got him to bed, but it's like the whole left side of his body isn't working. Then I mounted Sweet Ainsley, the only mule we have left these days, and rode to fetch *Señora* Dolores and Tori, hoping they can tend to Pa while I ride to Mesilla and bring that lousy sawbones.

Please, God, don't let Pa die before I get back.

October 30, 1863

The Velásquez family has been staying with me, even spending the night, forgetting the curse of this place. The doctor said Pa suffered what he called a cerebral apoplexy. He doesn't believe that Pa will live to see Thanksgiving, but this is the same pill-roller who told me Pa would die after that old Mexican sawed off his arm.

He can't talk, Pa, and Tori has to spoon breakfast and supper down his throat, clean him. Breaks my heart seeing him this way.

I. . . .

November 7, 1863

No change in Pa.

January 1, 1864

We've been trying to communicate with Pa some other way. His left side doesn't work, but that's the stump of his arm, so, yesterday morning, I put a pencil in his right hand and a scrap of paper on the Bible, asked him if he needed anything, and he blinked a few times—wasn't certain he understood—then scrawled out, NO.

Funny how glad that made Tori and I feel, and then Pa wrote something else. THANKS.

FORGIV

January 12, 1864

That's Pa's handwriting above here. He scribbled it today. I can't write about it just right now.

January 15, 1864

About Pa's one-word message: *Señora* Dolores had gone home to get some supplies, Tori was off somewhere, and I was oiling the Kerr revolver when Pa got all agitated, trying to talk, but only grunting, slobbering, and slapping his hand on the side of the bed.

"What is it?" I felt so useless, trying to understand

him. Frustrated, he pointed, and I spotted the pencil. Urgently I put it in his hand, wrapped his fingers tightly around it, looked around for some paper, couldn't find anything, and at last I saw this diary. I turned to the blank page, and he went to work, moaning, desperate. Stepping away from him, I called out for Tori, wherever she was, frightened as I've never been frightened before, and, a moment later, the pencil fell on the floor, and Pa drifted off to sleep.

Tori ran in as I picked up the paper and my diary. She looked at the word, then at me, finally at Pa. A few hours ago, she talked me into letting her saddle up Sweet Ainsley and ride to La Mesilla.

To fetch the priest.

January 28, 1864

Father Miguel has come and gone, did the best he could with the last rites and all. I hope Pa don't mind, us never being raised Catholic. The Mesilla doctor came by, too, and left, said it's a matter of time now. Pa's asleep, has been since he wrote that lone word.

February 11, 1864

It's over.

February 13, 1864

Sunday. Alone at breakfast, I poured coffee, looked at the bowl of stew *Señora* Dolores had left me, pushed it away, and told myself I must say a Bible verse before eating. I started talking, tears falling down my face.

" 'Man that is born of a woman is of few days and full of trouble. He cometh forth like a flower, and is cut down: he fleeth also as a shadow, and continueth not. And doth thou open thine eyes upon such an one, and bringest me into judgment with thee?' "

Two days ago, I found Pa in his bed, eyes open but not seeing, his flesh so cold, and cursed myself, blamed myself. He'd died while I slept. Well, *Señor* Vee calls it a blessing and—it really is—and a wonder Pa's heart hadn't given out months, or even years, ago. He looked older than Methuselah. Wasn't but 45.

I always thought Pa's funeral would bring in tons of mourners, but it was just me and Tori and her parents. We buried him in the little cemetery, away from that old dragoon who'd killed himself, away from those two soldiers shot down in the stagecoach robbery, away from where we'd first planted that old German captain. *Señor* Vee and his wife left me there for a while, to say good bye, and then Tori started pulling on my arm, begging me to come with her.

"The devil owns this place," she said. "Always, it cursed. It kill you, too, if you no leave. Get out, Smith. Get out. Please, for God's sake, you must go, for your own sake."

I just laughed, and she looked at me funny—no, scared—and I told her I had to wait here, had to wait for Julian.

"Perhaps he dead," she said, but I shook my head.

"He promised." Oh, I could just picture my brother, see him as clear as if it were yesterday, on our way back to Soldier's Farewell from the Velásquez place, him whispering while I cried.

Mark my words, Innis Smith Munro. I won't get killed. I promise you that.

She's gone. Practically flew from the cemetery, said she'd pray for me, ran.

I don't think she'll ever come back.

April 29, 1865

My Lord, has it been this long since last I've written in these pages? The war is over, the Union preserved, the Rebels whipped. I wait for Julian.

July 24, 1865

The prodigal son is home. Walked up 10 minutes ago, and looks as if he has been on the ankle express forever. Savage. Thin as a rail. Bearded, dirty, one butternut sleeve pinned up at his left shoulder. Stepping out of what's left of the stable after feeding the one mule left, I almost didn't recognize him. Didn't recognize him, not really, until he asked: "Where's Pa?"

Unable to speak, I pointed. He looked, not comprehending, then his knees buckled and I thought he'd fall, but he started walking. Going to the cemetery.

I must close this journal, grab the Kerr .45, and follow.

Same day, late evening

Just enough pages left in this journal to finish my story.

Heart racing, I left the house with the big revolver in my right hand, and took the trail to the grave-yard, stopping beside the old captain's former grave, sweating like I'd never sweated before, staring at that ragged figure standing over Pa's grave.

A few months after Pa's death—a lifetime ago—*Señor* Vee had placed a marble cross over Pa's grave. Nothing fancy, just a cross, not even a name chiseled into the stone, but the only marker of any kind in this cemetery.

My hand wouldn't stop shaking, and that .45 never felt so heavy. Ahead of me, Julian sobbed a bit, and slowly turned to face me, to die.

The wind blew harder, kicking up whirlwinds of dust.

The Kerr fell into the dirt.

That wasn't my brother I saw standing there. The beard. The one arm. So frail, so foreign. I saw my father, and then saw nothing but tears.

"How?" Julian managed to choke out the question. "When?"

Blocking the tears, the pain, I straightened. "Was a year ago February." I shook my head. "He just give out. Wore out."

If he noticed the Kerr, Julian never spoke of it, merely turned back to Pa's grave, and then he was on his knees, bawling like a newborn babe, wailing in such miserable torment, choking out things like: "It's my fault . . . I'm so sorry. . . ." And a broken word that chilled me:

"Forgive. . . ."

I don't remember walking up to him, don't remember putting my hands on his shoulders, but there I stood, hearing words from some strange voice, far away. My voice!

"He never held any grudge against you."

Julian looked up, his face so gaunt, red-rimmed eyes so . . . I don't know a word that can describe them. "I failed him, Smith."

The numbing, humbling truth of what I was about to say shook me, but I had to be strong. "No. I failed him. You did what you thought was right."

His trembling head shook, and he looked back at that cross. "No. I was wrong."

"We were both wrong," I said, thinking Pa had been wrong, too, only he knew it. "Let's go back to the house. Get out of the wind. A monsoon's blowing up."

The rain fell in torrents as I filled his cup with chicory and sat across from him.

"What kept you here?" he asked.

I started to answer, but couldn't, realizing I had left that revolver outside at the grave, chilled at how hate had driven me for four years. I wondered about that last word Pa wrote, wondered if he had been asking for forgiveness, had forgiven Julian, or was begging me to forgive. Forgive who? Julian? Pa? Myself?

I saw no need in telling my brother how Breed had came close to killing us both, or that Pa had spent his last few years as a walking whiskey vat. It didn't seem to matter. Nothing mattered.

Julian changed the subject. "How's Mr. Velásquez and his family?"

"Haven't heard from them in a spell. Alyvia got married, though."

He nodded as if he knew. We drank coffee. The rain fell. The roof leaked. The wind wailed.

"What?" My throat felt dry, and the wind brought a chill into the cabin. I pointed to the pinned up sleeve. "Happened?"

"Franklin," he said. "Big battle in Tennessee. Battle!" He spit out a mirthless laugh. "Wasn't anything short of murder, and I don't blame the Yanks who took my arm. It was our fool general, Hood." The head bowed, slowly shook again. "He got his whole army slaughtered." He was looking at me now as he spoke. "I learned something, Smith. The Confederate officers . . . some of them, at least . . . were no better than the Union martinets I fought with out West."

"You didn't join Wade Hampton?"

"No." He brushed away a tear. "Pa saw to that. Wrote Hampton a letter. When I got to South Carolina, requested the honor of joining Hampton's Legion, Hampton said he had heard of my atrocities . . . that's his word . . . my betrayal of family and honor. Hampton wouldn't have me. Almost challenged me to a duel. Said I wasn't fit to serve under any Southern command. No, Smith, you'll find no record of a Julian Munro anywhere in the Confederate Army. I enlisted under another name. Fought with the 1st Texas."

"What . . . ?" My head dropped, but I had to know. "And the money you took?"

He blurted out his answer, then stopped to regain his composure. "Pa was right about that, too!" The storm had stopped when he continued. "After we left here, after Breed rejoined us, Cassady sent Howell on to Burchville. My mule had thrown a shoe, so Howell and I switched mounts, figured he could nurse Sweet Ainsley to the mining camps. Later, he sent Breed back to watch our back trail. I didn't understand until later that Cassady had paid off those two. The rest of us rode to Santa Rita, then took a trail through the mountains to the river. I don't know what became of Breed or Howell."

I didn't tell him.

"And the others?"

"We also split up. Cassady took most of the money, rode up the river toward Santa Fé. Pinto and I started across the Jornado. I guess by then I had my suspicions, but . . . well, I'd crossed the Rubicon. Pinto knew the country. I don't know how. I was such an idiot. We hit the Pecos, turned south for Texas, rode to Fort Davis. The Yanks had abandoned her by then. That's when I knew for certain that I'd been played for a fool. Pinto kept riding for Mexico, and I . . . well . . . I lit out for Carolina. Maybe I should have turned myself in, but . . . ."

"And Cassady? Pinto?"

Julian shrugged. "For all I know Pinto's still in Mexico, rich. You remember Richardson Day, that lieutenant?"

I nodded, but didn't inform him of his friend's fate, either.

"I met his brother, campaigning in Georgia. He was a captain with the Second Kentucky Mounted Infantry. Kenny told me a story he'd heard about some rich Southerner who showed up in Denver City in the spring of '61 and opened a gambling hall before being run out of town by Unionists. He was killed, they say, by Cheyenne Indians on his way to Kansas in '63. That could have been Cassady. I'd like to think it was. Can't be sure, though."

There was another question I had to ask, for my brother, and for me.

"What's next?"

He finished his coffee, and rose. "I'll drift." He stood in the doorway, staring outside. The ground, the air smelled new. "Tucson, maybe. California. Oregon. Maybe. . . ." Turning to me, he said: "You've grown. Taller than me now." His eyes hardened, but just as quickly softened. "I thought you'd kill me." He stood a little straighter. "Nobody would blame you. Not even me."

"Pa would," I said, and we both knew it was true. "And I don't want to kill you, Jules." Not any more, I thought.

Oh, it wasn't that we could ever go back to how things had been, me the doting kid brother, him the strong one I'd admired and envied. He had been wrong, but I'd been wronger, letting hate drive me so. Maybe if I hadn't been so consumed, so blind, I could have pulled Pa back on his feet, stopped the drinking, made him raise mules, or I could have hauled him far away from these cursed ruins. I'm not sure I really forgave my brother, certainly couldn't bring myself to shake his hand. That would take time.

After a long while, still staring outside, he asked: "What are your plans?"

What about me? Suddenly I longed to see Tori, to beg her forgiveness, and then I got another notion. Crazy, maybe. Forlorn. But. . . .

Take up where Pa left off. Become a jackstock man. Maybe, maybe I could go to work for *Señor* Vee. He couldn't get around well, could use some help, and a smart man could learn a lot from Alejondro Velásquez. Besides, I could teach him about mules, teach him some of what Pa taught me. I'd leave Soldier's Farewell to the desert, to its ghosts. I'd left all the hate I had, left it with that unfired pistol up at the cemetery.

I never answered my brother, but I knew then what I'd do. I'd shave, clean myself up, get things in order. Maybe *Señor* Vee will banish me. Maybe Tori will send me packing. I wouldn't blame either of them. *Vamos a ver.* We shall see.

"Good bye." Julian walked outside.

"Take the mule!" I called out suddenly, unexpectedly, and he stopped, but never looked back. "She's yours anyway," I said. "It's Sweet Ainsley."

After another long pause, he shook his head, his voice breaking again. "You'll need her."

"No." I pictured myself at the Velásquez place, pitching my proposal to *Señor* Vee, and maybe, God willing, in a few years making another proposal. "I'll walk. I don't have far to go."

Acknowledgments

Special thanks to the New Mexico State Archives, the Santa Fe and Vista Grande public libraries, and Butterfield-Overland historian, Melody Groves, of Albuquerque, New Mexico, for research help with this novel.

And to my son, Jack, who kept an eye out for rattle-snakes while I scouted out the southern New Mexico locales in this novel around Soldier's Farewell, Besse Rhodes (Bessie Rhoads on today's maps), and elsewhere between Gage and White Signal in Luna and Grant counties.

Recommended reading about the John Butterfield's Overland Mail Company includes *That Old Overland Stagecoaching* by Eva Jolene Boyd (Republic of Texas Press, 1993); *The Butterfield Overland Mail*, three volumes, by Roscoe and Margaret Conkling (Arthur H. Clark, 1947); *The Butterfield Trail in New Mexico* by George Hackler (Yucca Enterprises, 2005); *The Butterfield Overland Mail* by Waterman L. Ormsby, edited by Lyle H. Wright and Josephine M. Bynum (The Huntington Library, 1942); and *A Compendium of The Overland Mail Company On the South Route, 1858–1861 and the Period Surrounding It* by G.C. Tompkins (Talna Corp, 1985).

About the Author

Johnny D. Boggs has worked cattle, shot rapids in a canoe, hiked across mountains and deserts, traipsed around ghost towns, and spent hours poring over microfilm in library archives—all in the name of finding a good story. He's also one of the few Western writers to have won two Spur Awards from Western Writers of America (for his novel, *Camp Ford*, in 2006, and his short story, "A Piano at Dead Man's Crossing", in 2002) and the Western Heritage Wrangler Award from the National Cowboy and Western Heritage Museum (for his novel, *Spark on the Prairie: The Trial of the Kiowa Chiefs*, in 2004). A native of South Carolina, Boggs spent almost fifteen years in Texas as a journalist at the *Dallas Times Herald* and *Fort Worth Star-Telegram* before moving to New Mexico in 1998 to concentrate full time on his novels. Author of dozens of published short stories, he has also written for more than fifty newspapers and magazines, and is a frequent contributor to *Boys' Life*, *New Mexico Magazine*, *Persimmon Hill*, and *True West*. His Western novels cover a wide range. *The Lonesome Chisholm Trail* is an authentic cattle-drive story, while *Lonely Trumpet* is an historical novel about the first black graduate of West Point. *The Despoilers* and *Ghost Legion* are set in the Carolina backcountry during the Revolutionary War. *The Big Fifty* chronicles the slaughter of buffalo on the southern plains in the 1870s, while *East of the Border* is a comedy about the theatrical offerings of Buffalo

Bill Cody, Wild Bill Hickok, and Texas Jack Omohundro, and *Camp Ford* tells about a Civil War baseball game between Union prisoners of war and Confederate guards. "Boggs's narrative voice captures the old-fashioned style of the past," *Publishers Weekly* said, and *Booklist* called him "among the best Western writers at work today." Boggs lives with his wife Lisa and son Jack in Santa Fé. His Web site is www.johnnydboggs.com.

☐ **YES!**

Sign me up for the Leisure Western Book Club and send my FREE BOOKS! If I choose to stay in the club, I will pay only $14.00* each month, a savings of $9.96!

NAME: _____

ADDRESS: _____

TELEPHONE: _____

EMAIL: _____

☐ I want to pay by credit card.

☐ **VISA**   ☐ **MasterCard.**   ☐ **DISCOVER**

ACCOUNT #: _____

EXPIRATION DATE: _____

SIGNATURE: _____

Mail this page along with $2.00 shipping and handling to:
Leisure Western Book Club
PO Box 6640
Wayne, PA 19087
Or fax (must include credit card information) to:
610-995-9274
You can also sign up online at **www.dorchesterpub.com**.
*Plus $2.00 for shipping. Offer open to residents of the U.S. and Canada only.
Canadian residents please call 1-800-481-9191 for pricing information.
If under 18, a parent or guardian must sign. Terms, prices and conditions subject to
change. Subscription subject to acceptance. Dorchester Publishing reserves the right
to reject any order or cancel any subscription.